L-50

D1424053

THE
MURDER BOOK
OF J.G. REEDER

THE
MURDER BOOK
OF J.G. REEDER

Edgar Wallace

Dover Publications, Inc.
NEW YORK

This Dover edition, first published in 1982, is an unabridged republication of the edition published by the A. L. Burt Company, N.Y., n.d. (first publication: Hodder & Stoughton, London, 1925, as *The Mind of Mr. J. G. Reeder*).

Manufactured in the United States of America
Dover Publications, Inc., 180 Varick Street, New York, N.Y. 10014

Library of Congress Cataloging in Publication Data

Wallace, Edgar, 1875-1932.
  The murder book of J.G. Reeder.

  Reprint. Originally published: Garden City, N.Y. : Published for the Crime Club by Doubleday, Doran, 1929.
  I. Title.
PR6045.A327M8 1982   823'.912   82-9486
ISBN 0-486-24374-5   AACR2

Contents

Contents

THE
MURDER BOOK
OF J.G. REEDER

I

The Poetical Policeman

The day Mr. Reeder arrived at the Public Prosecutor's office was indeed a day of fate for Mr. Lambton Green, branch manager of the London Scottish and Midland Bank.

That branch of the bank which Mr. Green controlled was situate at the corner of Pell Street and Firling Avenue on the "country side" of Ealing. It was a fairly large building and, unlike most suburban branch offices, the whole of the premises were devoted to banking business, for the bank carried very heavy deposits, the Lunar Traction Company, with three thousand people on its payroll, the Associated Novelties Corporation, with its enormous turnover, and the Laraphone Company being only three of the L.S.M.'s customers.

On Wednesday afternoons, in preparation for the pay days of these corporations, large sums in currency were brought from the head office and deposited in the steel and concrete strong-room, which was immediately beneath Mr. Green's private office, but admission to which was gained through a steel door in the general office. This door was observable from the street, and to assist observation there was a shaded lamp fixed to the wall immediately above, which threw a powerful beam of light upon the door. Further security was ensured by the employment of a night watchman, Arthur Malling, an army pensioner.

The bank lay on a restricted police beat which had been so arranged that the constable on patrol passed the bank every forty minutes. It was his practice to look through the window and exchange signals with the night watchman, his orders being to wait until Malling appeared.

On the night of October 17th Police-Constable Burnett stopped as usual before the wide peep-hole and glanced into the bank. The first thing he noticed was that the lamp above the strong-room door had been extinguished. The night watchman was not visible, and, his suspicions aroused, the officer did not wait for the man to put in an appearance as he would ordinarily have done, but passed the window to the door, which, to his alarm, he found ajar. Pushing it open, he entered the bank, calling Malling by name. There was no answer.

Permeating the air was a faint, sweet scent which he could not locate. The general offices were empty and, entering the manager's room in which a light burnt, he saw a figure stretched upon the ground. It was the night watchman. His wrists were handcuffed, two straps had been tightly buckled about his knees and ankles.

The explanation for the strange and sickly aroma was now clear. Above the head of the prostrate man was suspended, by a wire hooked to the picture-rail, an old tin can, the bottom of which was perforated so that there fell an incessant trickle of some volatile liquid upon the thick cotton pad which covered Malling's face.

Burnett, who had been wounded in the war, had instantly recognised the smell of chloroform and, dragging the unconscious man into the outer office, snatched the pad from his face and, leaving him only long enough to telephone to the police station, sought vainly to bring him to consciousness.

The police reserves arrived within a few minutes, and with them the divisional surgeon who, fortunately, had been at the station when the alarm came through. Every effort to restore the unfortunate man to life proved unavailing.

"He was probably dead when he was found," was the police doctor's verdict. "What those scratches are on his right palm is a mystery."

He pulled open the clenched fist and showed half a dozen little scratches. They were recent, for there was a smear of blood on the palm.

Burnett was sent at once to arouse Mr. Green, the manager, who lived in Firling Avenue, at the corner of which the bank stood; a street of semi-detached villas of a pattern familiar enough to the Londoner. As the officer walked through the little front garden to the door he saw a light through the panels, and he had hardly knocked before the door was opened and Mr. Lambton Green appeared, fully dressed and, to the officer's discerning eye, in a state of considerable agitation. Constable Burnett saw on a hall chair a big bag, a travelling rug and an umbrella.

The little manager listened, pale as death, while Burnett told him of his discovery.

"The bank robbed? Impossible!" he almost shrieked. "My God! this is awful!"

He was so near the point of collapse that Burnett had to assist him into the street.

"I—I was going away on a holiday," he said incoherently, as he walked up the dark thoroughfare toward the bank premises. "The fact is—I was leaving the bank. I left a note—explaining to the directors."

Into a circle of suspicious men the manager tottered. He unlocked the drawer of his desk, looked and crumbled up.

"They're not here!" he said wildly. "I left them here—my keys—with the note!"

And then he swooned. When the dazed man recovered he found himself in a police cell and, later in the day, he drooped before a police magistrate, supported by two constables, and listened, like a man in a dream, to a charge of causing the death of Arthur Malling, and further, of converting to his own use the sum of £100,000.

It was on the morning of the first remand that Mr. John G. Reeder, with some reluctance for he was suspicious of all Government departments, transferred himself from his own office on Lower Regent Street to a somewhat gloomy bureau on the top floor of the building which housed the Public Prosecutor. In making this change he advanced only one stipulation: that he should be connected by private telephone wire with his old bureau.

He did not demand this—he never demanded anything. He asked, nervously and apologetically. There was a certain wistful helplessness about John G. Reeder that made people feel sorry for him, that caused even the Public Prosecutor a few uneasy moments of doubt as to whether he had been quite wise in substituting this weak-appearing man of middle age for Inspector Holford—bluff, capable, and heavily mysterious.

Mr. Reeder was something over fifty, a long-faced gentleman with sandy-grey hair and a slither of side whiskers that mercifully distracted attention from his large outstanding ears. He wore halfway down his nose a pair of steel-rimmed pince-nez, through which nobody had ever seen him look—they were invariably removed when he was reading. A high and flat-crowned bowler hat matched and yet did not match a frock-coat tightly buttoned across his sparse chest. His boots were square-toed, his cravat—of the broad, chest-protector pattern—was ready-made and buckled into place behind a Gladstonian collar. The neatest appendage to Mr. Reeder was an umbrella rolled so tightly that it might be mistaken for a frivolous walking cane. Rain or shine, he carried this article hooked to his arm, and within living memory it had never been unfurled.

Inspector Holford (promoted now to the responsibilities of Superintendent) met him in the office to hand over his duties, and a more tangible quantity in the shape of old furniture and fixings.

"Glad to know you, Mr. Reeder. I haven't had the pleasure of meeting you before, but I've heard a lot about you. You've been doing Bank of England work, haven't you?"

Mr. Reeder whispered that he had had that honour, and sighed as though he regretted the drastic sweep of fate that had torn him from the obscurity of his labours. Mr. Holford's scrutiny was full of misgivings.

"Well," he said awkwardly, "this job is different, though I'm told that you are one of the best informed men in London, and if that is the case this will be easy work. Still, we've never had an outsider—I mean, so to speak, a private detective—in this office before, and naturally the Yard is a bit——''

"I quite understand," murmured Mr. Reeder, hanging up his immaculate umbrella. "It is very natural. Mr. Bolond expected the appointment. His wife is annoyed—very properly. But she has no reason to be. She is an ambitious woman. She has a third interest in a West End dancing club that might be raided one of these days."

Holford was staggered. Here was news that was little more than a whispered rumour at Scotland Yard.

"How the devil do you know that?" he blurted.

Mr. Reeder's smile was one of self-depreciation.

"One picks up odd scraps of information," he said apologetically. "I—I see wrong in everything. That is my curious perversion—I have a criminal mind!"

Holford drew a long breath.

"Well—there is nothing much doing. That Ealing case is pretty clear. Green is an ex-convict, who got a job at the bank during the war and worked up to manager. He has done seven years for conversion."

"Embezzlement and conversion," murmured Mr. Reeder. "I—er—I'm afraid I was the principal witness against him: bank crimes were rather—er —a hobby of mine. Yes, he got into difficulties with money-lenders. Very foolish—extremely foolish. And he doesn't admit his error." Mr. Reeder sighed heavily. "Poor fellow! With his life at stake one may forgive and indeed condone his pitiful prevarications."

The inspector stared at the new man in amazement.

"I don't know that there is much 'poor fellow' about him. He has cached £100,000 and told the weakest yarn that I've ever read—you'll find copies of the police reports here, if you'd like to read them. The scratches on Malling's hand are curious—they've found several on the other hand. They are not deep enough to suggest a struggle. As to the yarn that Green tells——"

Mr. J. G. Reeder nodded sadly.

"It was not an ingenious story," he said, almost with regret. "If I remember rightly, his story was something like this: he had been recognised by a man who served in Dartmoor with him, and this fellow wrote a blackmailing letter telling him to pay or clear out. Sooner than return to a life of crime, Green wrote out all the facts to his directors, put the letter in the drawer of his desk with his keys, and left a note for his head cashier on the desk itself, intending to leave London and try to make a fresh start where he was unknown."

"There were no letters in or on the desk, and no keys," said the inspector decisively. "The only true part of the yarn was that he had done time."

"Imprisonment," suggested Mr. Reeder plaintively. He had a horror of slang. "Yes, that was true."

Left alone in his office, he spent a very considerable time at his private telephone, communing with the young person who was still a young person, although the passage of time had dealt unkindly with her. For the rest of the morning he was reading the depositions which his predecessor had put on the desk.

It was late in the afternoon when the Public Prosecutor strolled into his room and glanced at the big pile of manuscript through which his subordinate was wading.

"What are you reading—the Green business?" he asked, with a note of satisfaction in his voice. "I'm glad that is interesting you—though it seems a fairly straightforward case. I have had a letter from the president of the man's bank, who for some reason seems to think Green was telling the truth."

Mr. Reeder looked up with that pained expression of his which he invariably wore when he was puzzled.

"Here is the evidence of Policeman Burnett," he said. "Perhaps you can enlighten me, sir. Policeman Burnett stated in his evidence—let me read it:

"Some time before I reached the bank premises I saw a man standing at the corner of the street, immediately outside the bank. I saw him distinctly in the light of a passing mail van. I did not attach any importance to his presence, and I did not see him again. It was possible for this man to have gone round the block and come to 120 Firling Avenue without being seen by me. Immediately after I saw him, my foot struck against a piece of iron on the sidewalk. I put my lamp on the object and found it was an old horseshoe; I had seen children playing with this particular shoe earlier in the evening. When I looked again towards the corner, the man had disappeared. He would have seen the light of my lamp. I saw no other person, and so far as I can remember, there was no light showing in Green's house when I passed it."

Mr. Reeder looked up.

"Well?" said the Prosecutor. "There's nothing remarkable about that. It was probably Green, who dodged round the block and came in at the back of the constable."

Mr. Reeder scratched his chin.

"Yes," he said thoughtfully, "ye-es." He shifted uncomfortably in his chair. "Would it be considered indecorous if I made a few inquiries, independent of the police?" he asked nervously. "I should not like them to think that a mere dilettante was interfering with their lawful functions."

"By all means," said the Prosecutor heartily. "Go down and see the officer in charge of the case: I'll give you a note to him—it is by no means unusual for my officer to conduct a separate investigation, though I am afraid you will discover very little. The ground has been well covered by Scotland Yard."

"It would be permissible to see the man?" hesitated Reeder.

"Green? Why, of course! I will send you up the necessary order."

The light was fading from a grey, blustering sky, and rain was falling fitfully, when Mr. Reeder, with his furled umbrella hooked to his arm, his coat collar turned up, stepped through the dark gateway of Brixton Prison and was led to the cell where a distracted man sat, his head upon his hands, his pale eyes gazing into vacancy.

"It's true; it's true! Every word." Green almost sobbed the words.

A pallid man, inclined to be bald, with a limp yellow moustache, going grey. Reeder, with his extraordinary memory for faces, recognised him the moment he saw him, though it was some time before the recognition was mutual.

"Yes, Mr. Reeder, I remember you now. You were the gentleman who caught me before. But I've been as straight as a die. I've never taken a farthing that didn't belong to me. What my poor girl will think——"

"Are you married?" asked Mr. Reeder sympathetically.

"No, but I was going to be—rather late in life. She's nearly thirty years younger than me, and the best girl that ever . . ."

Reeder listened to the rhapsody that followed, the melancholy deepening in his face.

"She hasn't been into the court, thank God, but she knows the truth. A friend of mine told me that she has been absolutely knocked out."

"Poor soul!" Mr. Reeder shook his head.

"It happened on her birthday, too," the man went on bitterly.

"Did she know you were going away?"

"Yes, I told her the night before. I'm not going to bring her into the case. If we'd been properly engaged it would be different; but she's married and is divorcing her husband, but the decree hasn't been made absolute yet. That's why I never went about with her or saw much of her. And of course, nobody knew about our engagement, although we lived in the same street."

"Firling Avenue?" asked Reeder, and the bank manager nodded despondently.

"She was married when she was seventeen to a brute. It was pretty galling for me, having to keep quiet about it—I mean, for nobody to know about our engagement. All sorts of rotten people were making up to her, and I had just to grind my teeth and say nothing. Impossible people! Why, that fool Burnett, who arrested me, he was sweet on her; used to write her poetry—you wouldn't think it possible in a policeman, would you?''

The outrageous incongruity of a poetical policeman did not seem to shock the detective.

"There is poetry in every soul, Mr. Green," he said gently, "and a policeman is a man.''

Though he dismissed the eccentricity of the constable so lightly, the poetical policeman filled his mind all the way home to his house in the Brockley Road, and occupied his thoughts for the rest of his waking time.

It was a quarter to eight o'clock in the morning and the world seemed entirely populated by milkmen and whistling newspaper boys, when Mr. J. G. Reeder came into Firling Avenue.

He stopped only for a second outside the bank, which had long since ceased to be an object of local awe and fearfulness, and pursued his way down the broad avenue. On either side of the thoroughfare ran a row of pretty villas—pretty although they bore a strong family resemblance to one another; each house with its little fore-court, sometimes laid out simply as a grass plot, sometimes decorated with flower-beds. Green's house was the eighteenth in the road on the right-hand side. Here he had lived with a cook-housekeeper, and apparently gardening was not his hobby, for the fore-court was covered with grass that had been allowed to grow at its will.

Before the twenty-sixth house in the road Mr. Reeder paused and gazed with mild interest at the blue blinds which covered every window. Evidently Miss Magda Grayne was a lover of flowers, for geraniums filled the window-boxes and were set at intervals along the tiny border under the bow window. In the centre of the grass plot was a circular flower-bed with one flowerless rose tree, the leaves of which were drooping and brown.

As he raised his eyes to the upper window, the blind went up slowly, and he was dimly conscious that there was a figure behind the white lace curtains. Mr. Reeder walked hurriedly away, as one caught in an immodest act, and resumed his peregrinations until he came to the big nursery gardener's which formed the corner lot at the far end of the road.

Here he stood for some time in contemplation, his arm resting on the iron railings, his eyes staring blankly at the vista of greenhouses. He remained in this attitude so long that one of the nurserymen, not unnaturally thinking that a stranger was seeking a way into the gardens, came over with the laborious gait of the man who wrings his living from the soil, and asked if he was wanting anybody.

"Several people," sighed Mr. Reeder; "several people!"

Leaving the resentful man to puzzle out his impertinence, he slowly retraced his steps. At No. 412 he stopped again, opened the little iron gate and passed up the path to the front door. A small girl answered his knock and ushered him into the parlour.

The room was not well furnished; it was scarcely furnished at all. A strip of almost new linoleum covered the passage; the furniture of the parlour itself was made up of wicker chairs, a square of art carpet and a table. He heard the sound of feet above his head, feet on bare boards, and then presently the door opened and a girl came in.

She was pretty in a heavy way, but on her face he saw the marks of sorrow. It was pale and haggard; the eyes looked as though she had been recently weeping.

"Miss Magda Grayne?" he asked, rising as she came in.

She nodded.

"Are you from the police?" she asked quickly.

"Not exactly the police," he corrected carefully. "I hold an—er—an appointment in the office of the Public Prosecutor, which is analogous to, but distinct from, a position in the Metropolitan Police Force."

She frowned, and then:

"I wondered if anybody would come to see me," she said. "Mr. Green sent you?"

"Mr. Green told me of your existence: he did not send me."

There came to her face in that second a look which almost startled him. Only for a fleeting space of time, the expression had dawned and passed almost before the untrained eye could detect its passage.

"I was expecting somebody to come," she said. Then: "What made him do it?" she asked.

"You think he is guilty?"

"The police think so." She drew a long sigh. "I wish to God I had never seen—this place!"

He did not answer; his eyes were roving round the apartment. On a bamboo table was an old vase which had been clumsily filled with golden chrysanthemums, of a peculiarly beautiful variety. Not all, for amidst them flowered a large Michaelmas daisy that had the forlorn appearance of a parvenu that had strayed by mistake into noble company.

"You're fond of flowers?" he murmured.

She looked at the vase indifferently.

"Yes, I like flowers," she said. "The girl put them in there." Then: "Do you think they will hang him?"

The brutality of the question, put without hesitation, pained Reeder.

"It is a very serious charge," he said. And then: "Have you a photograph of Mr. Green?"

She frowned.

"Yes; do you want it?"

8

He nodded.

She had hardly left the room before he was at the bamboo table and had lifted out the flowers. As he had seen through the glass, they were roughly tied with a piece of string. He examined the ends, and here again his first observation had been correct: none of these flowers had been cut; they had been plucked bodily from their stalks. Beneath the string was the paper which had been first wrapped about the stalks. It was a page torn from a notebook; he could see the red lines, but the pencilled writing was indecipherable.

As her foot sounded on the stairs, he replaced the flowers in the vase, and when she came in he was looking through the window into the street.

"Thank you," he said, as he took the photograph from her.

It bore an affectionate inscription on the back.

"You're married, he tells me, madam?"

"Yes, I am married, and practically divorced," she said shortly.

"Have you been living here long?"

"About three months," she answered. "It was his wish that I should live here."

He looked at the photograph again.

"Do you know Constable Burnett?"

He saw a dull flush come to her face and die away again.

"Yes, I know the sloppy fool!" she said viciously. And then, realising that she had been surprised into an expression which was not altogether ladylike, she went on, in a softer tone: "Mr. Burnett is rather sentimental, and I don't like sentimental people, especially—well, you understand, Mr.——"

"Reeder," murmured that gentleman.

"You understand, Mr. Reeder, that when a girl is engaged and in my position, those kind of attentions are not very welcome."

Reeder was looking at her keenly. Of her sorrow and distress there could be no doubt. On the subject of the human emotions, and the ravages they make upon the human countenance, Mr. Reeder was almost as great an authority as Mantegazza.

"On your birthday," he said. "How very sad! You were born on the seventeenth of October. You are English, of course?"

"Yes, I'm English," she said shortly. "I was born in Walworth—in Wallington. I once lived in Walworth."

"How old are you?"

"Twenty-three," she answered.

Mr. Reeder took off his glasses and polished them on a large silk handkerchief.

"The whole thing is inexpressibly sad," he said. "I am glad to have had

9

the opportunity of speaking with you, young lady. I sympathise with you very deeply."

And in this unsatisfactory way he took his departure.

She closed the door on him, saw him stop in the middle of the path and pick up something from a border bed, and wondered, frowning, why this middle-aged man had picked up the horseshoe she had thrown through the window the night before. Into Mr. Reeder's tail pocket went this piece of rusted steel and then he continued his thoughtful way to the nursery gardens, for he had a few questions to ask.

The men of Section 10 were parading for duty when Mr. Reeder came timidly into the charge room and produced his credentials to the inspector in charge.

"Oh, yes, Mr. Reeder," said that officer affably. "We have had a note from the P. P.'s office, and I think I had the pleasure of working with you on that big slush* case a few years ago. Now what can I do for you? . . . Burnett? Yes, he's here."

He called the man's name and a young and good-looking officer stepped from the ranks.

"He's the man who discovered the murder—he's marked for promotion," said the inspector. "Burnett, this gentleman is from the Public Prosecutor's office and he wants a little talk with you. Better use my office, Mr. Reeder."

The young policeman saluted and followed the shuffling figure into the privacy of the inspector's office. He was a confident young man: already his name and portrait had appeared in the newspapers, the hint of promotion had become almost an accomplished fact, and before his eyes was the prospect of a supreme achievement.

"They tell me that you are something of a poet, officer," said Mr. Reeder.

Burnett blushed.

"Why, yes, sir. I write a bit," he confessed.

"Love poems, yes?" asked the other gently. "One finds time in the night—er—for such fancies. And there is no inspiration like—er—love, officer."

Burnett's face was crimson.

"I've done a bit of writing in the night, sir," he said, "though I've never neglected my duty."

"Naturally," murmured Mr. Reeder. "You have a poetical mind. It was a poetical thought to pluck flowers in the middle of the night——"

---

* Slush = forged Bank of England notes.

"The nurseryman told me I could take any flowers I wanted," Burnett interrupted hastily. "I did nothing wrong."

Reeder inclined his head in agreement.

"That I know. You picked the flowers in the dark—by the way, you inadvertently included a Michaelmas daisy with your chrysanthemums—tied up your little poem to them and left them on the doorstep with—er—a horseshoe. I wondered what had become of that horseshoe."

"I threw them up on to her—to the lady's window-sill," corrected the uncomfortable young man. "As a matter of fact, the idea didn't occur to me until I had passed the house——"

Mr. Reeder's face was thrust forward.

"This is what I want to confirm," he said softly. "The idea of leaving the flowers did not occur to you until you had passed her house? The horseshoe suggested the thought? Then you went back, picked the flowers, tied them up with the little poem you had already written, and tossed them up to her window—we need not mention the lady's name."

Constable Burnett's face was a study.

"I don't know how you guessed that, but it is a fact. If I've done anything wrong——"

"It is never wrong to be in love," said Mr. J. G. Reeder soberly. "Love is a very beautiful experience—I have frequently read about it."

Miss Magda Grayne had dressed to go out for the afternoon and was putting on her hat, when she saw the queer man who had called so early that morning walking up the tessellated path. Behind him she recognised a detective engaged in the case. The servant was out; nobody could be admitted except by herself. She walked quickly behind the dressing-table into the bay of the window and glanced up and down the road. Yes, there was the taxicab which usually accompanies such visitations, and, standing by the driver, another man, obviously a "busy."

She pulled up the overlay of her bed, took out the flat pad of bank-notes that she found, and thrust them into her handbag, then, stepping on tiptoe, she went out to the landing, into the unfurnished back room, and, opening the window, dropped to the flat roof of the kitchen. In another minute she was in the garden and through the back gate. A narrow passage divided the two lines of villas that backed on one another. She was in High Street and had boarded a car before Mr. Reeder grew tired of knocking. To the best of his knowledge Mr. Reeder never saw her again.

*   *   *   *   *   *

At the Public Prosecutor's request, he called at his chief's house after dinner and told his surprising story.

11

"Green, who had the unusual experience of being promoted to his position over the heads of his seniors, for special services he rendered during the war, was undoubtedly an ex-convict, and he spoke the truth when he said that he had received a letter from a man who had served a period of imprisonment with him. The name of this blackmailer is, or rather was, Arthur George Crater, whose other name was Malling!"

"Not the night watchman?" said the Public Prosecutor, in amazement.

Mr. Reeder nodded.

"Yes, sir, it was Arthur Malling. His daughter, Miss Magda Crater, was, as she very truly said, born at Walworth on the 17th of October, 1900. She said Wallington after, but Walworth first. One observes that when people adopt false family names, they seldom change their given names, and the 'Magda' was easy to identify.

"Evidently Malling had planned this robbery of the bank very carefully. He had brought his daughter, under a false name, to Ealing, and had managed to get her introduced to Mr. Green. Magda's job was to worm her way into Green's confidence and learn all that she could. Possibly it was part of her duty to secure casts of the keys. Whether Malling recognised in the manager an old prison acquaintance, or whether he obtained the facts from the girl, we shall never know. But when the information came to him, he saw, in all probability, an opportunity of robbing the bank and of throwing suspicion upon the manager.

"The girl's rôle was that of a woman who was to be divorced, and I must confess this puzzled me until I realised that in no circumstances would Malling wish his daughter's name to be associated with the bank manager.

"The night of the seventeenth was chosen for the raid. Malling's plan to get rid of the manager had succeeded. He saw the letter on the table in Green's private office, read it, secured the keys—although he had in all probability a duplicate set—and at a favourable moment cleared as much portable money from the bank vaults as he could carry, hurried them round to the house in Firling Avenue, where they were buried in the central bed of the front garden, under a rose bush—I rather imagined there was something interfering with the nutrition of that unfortunate bush the first time I saw it. I can only hope that the tree is not altogether dead, and I have given instructions that it shall be replanted and well fertilised."

"Yes, yes," said the Prosecutor, who was not at all interested in horticulture.

"In planting the tree, as he did in some haste, Malling scratched his hand. Roses have thorns—I went to Ealing to find the rose bush that had scratched his hand. Hurrying back to the bank, he waited, knowing that Constable Burnett was due at a certain time. He had prepared the can of chloroform, the handcuffs and straps were waiting for him, and he stood at the corner of the street until he saw the flash of Burnett's lamp; then, running into the bank and leaving the door ajar, he strapped himself, fastened the handcuffs and lay down, expecting that the policeman would arrive, find the open door and rescue him before much harm was done.

"But Constable Burnett had had some pleasant exchanges with the daughter. Doubtless she had received instructions from her father to be as pleasant to him as possible. Burnett was a poetical young man, knew it was her birthday, and as he walked along the street his foot struck an old horseshoe, and the idea occurred to him that he should return, attach the horseshoe to some flowers, which the nurseryman had given him permission to pick, and leave his little bouquet, so to speak, at his lady's feet—a poetical idea, and one worthy of the finest traditions of the Metropolitan Police Force. This he did, but it took some time; and all the while this young man was philandering—Arthur Crater was dying!

"In a few seconds after lying down he must have passed from consciousness . . . the chloroform still dripped, and when the policeman eventually reached the bank, ten minutes after he was due, the man was dead!"

The Public Prosecutor sat back in his padded chair and frowned at his new subordinate.

"How on earth did you piece together all this?" he asked in wonder.

Mr. Reeder shook his head sadly.

"I have that perversion," he said. "It is a terrible misfortune, but it is true. I see evil in everything . . . in dying rose bushes, in horseshoes—in poetry even. I have the mind of a criminal. It is deplorable!"

II

The Treasure Hunt

There is a tradition in criminal circles that even the humblest of detective officers is a man of wealth and substance, and that his secret hoard was secured by thieving, bribery, and blackmail. It is the gossip of the fields, the quarries, the tailor's shop, the laundry, and the bakehouse of fifty county prisons and three convict establishments, that all highly placed detectives have by nefarious means laid up for themselves sufficient earthly treasures to make work a hobby and their official pittance the most inconsiderable portion of their incomes.

Since Mr. J. G. Reeder had for more than twenty years dealt exclusively with bank robbers and forgers, who are the aristocrats and capitalists of the underworld, legend credited him with country houses and immense secret reserves. Not that he would have a great deal of money in the bank. It was admitted that he was too clever to risk discovery by the authorities. No, it was hidden somewhere: it was the pet dream of hundreds of unlawful men that they would some day discover the hoard and live happily ever after. The one satisfactory aspect of his affluence (they all agreed) was that, being an old man—he was over 50—he couldn't take his money with him, for gold melts at a certain temperature and gilt-edged stock is seldom printed on asbestos paper.

The Director of Public Prosecutions was lunching one Saturday at his club with a judge of the King's Bench—Saturday being one of the two days in the week when a judge gets properly fed. And the conversation drifted to a certain Mr. J. G. Reeder, the chief of the Director's sleuths.

"He's capable," he confessed reluctantly, "but I hate his hat. It is the sort that So-and-so used to wear," he mentioned by name an eminent politician; "and I loathe his black frock-coat—people who see him coming into the office think he's a coroner's officer—but he's capable. His side whiskers are an abomination, and I have a feeling that, if I talked rough to him, he would burst into tears—a gentle soul. Almost too gentle for my kind of work. He apologises to the messenger every time he rings for him!"

The judge, who knew something about humanity, answered with a frosty smile.

"He sounds rather like a potential murderer to me," he said cynically.

Here, in his extravagance, he did Mr. J. G. Reeder an injustice, for Mr. Reeder was incapable of breaking the law—quite. At the same time there were many people who formed an altogether wrong conception of J. G.'s harmlessness as an individual. And one of these was a certain Lew Kohl, who mixed bank-note printing with elementary burglary.

Threatened men live long, a trite saying but, like most things trite, true. In a score of cases, where Mr. J. G. Reeder had descended from the witness stand, he had met the baleful eye of the man in the dock and had listened with mild interest to divers promises as to what would happen to him in the near or the remote future. For he was a great authority on forged bank-notes and he had sent many men to penal servitude.

Mr. Reeder, that inoffensive man, had seen prisoners foaming at the mouth in their rage, he had seen them white and livid, he had heard their howling execrations and he had met these men after their release from prison and had found them amiable souls half ashamed and half amused at their nearly forgotten outbursts and horrific threats.

But when, in the early part of 1914, Lew Kohl was sentenced for ten years, he neither screamed his imprecations nor registered a vow to tear Mr. Reeder's heart, lungs, and important organs from his frail body.

Lew just smiled and his eyes caught the detective's for the space of a second—the forger's eyes were pale blue and speculative, and they held neither hate nor fury. Instead, they said in so many words:

"At the first opportunity I will kill you."

Mr. Reeder read the message and sighed heavily, for he disliked fuss of all kinds, and resented, in so far as he could resent anything, the injustice of being made personally responsible for the performance of a public duty.

Many years had passed, and considerable changes had occurred in Mr. Reeder's fortune. He had transferred from the specialised occupation of detecting the makers of forged bank-notes to the more general practice of the Public Prosecutor's bureau, but he never forgot Lew's smile.

The work in Whitehall was not heavy and it was very interesting. To Mr. Reeder came most of the anonymous letters which the Director received in shoals. In the main they were self-explanatory, and it required no particular intelligence to discover their motive. Jealousy, malice, plain mischief-making, and occasionally a sordid desire to benefit financially by the information which was conveyed, were behind the majority. But occasionally:

Sir James is going to marry his cousin, and it's not three months since his poor wife fell overboard from the Channel steamer crossing to Calais. There's something very fishy about this business. Miss Margaret doesn't like him, for she knows he's

15

after her money. Why was I sent away to London that night? He doesn't like driving in the dark, either. It's strange that he wanted to drive that night when it was raining like blazes.

This particular letter was signed "A Friend." Justice has many such friends.

"Sir James" was Sir James Tithermite, who had been a director of some new public department during the war and had received a baronetcy for his services.

"Look it up," said the Director when he saw the letter. "I seem to remember that Lady Tithermite was drowned at sea."

"On the nineteenth of December last year," said Mr. Reeder solemnly. "She and Sir James were going to Monte Carlo, breaking their journey in Paris. Sir James, who has a house near Maidstone, drove to Dover, garaging the car at the Lord Wilson Hotel. The night was stormy and the ship had a rough crossing—they were halfway across when Sir James came to the purser and said that he had missed his wife. Her baggage was in the cabin, her passport, rail ticket, and hat, but the lady was not found, indeed was never seen again."

The Director nodded.

"I see, you've read up the case."

"I remember it," said Mr. Reeder. "The case is a favourite speculation of mine. Unfortunately, I see evil in everything and I have often thought how easy—but I fear that I take a warped view of life. It is a horrible handicap to possess a criminal mind."

The Director looked at him suspiciously. He was never quite sure whether Mr. Reeder was serious. At that moment, his sobriety was beyond challenge.

"A discharged chauffeur wrote that letter, of course," he began.

"Thomas Dayford, of 179 Barrack Street, Maidstone," concluded Mr. Reeder. "He is at present in the employ of the Kent Motor-Bus Company, and has three children, two of whom are twins and bonny little rascals."

The Chief laughed helplessly.

"I'll take it that you *know!*" he said. "See what there is behind the letter. Sir James is a big fellow in Kent, a Justice of the Peace, and he has powerful political influences. There is nothing in this letter, of course. Go warily, Reeder—if any kick comes back to this office, it goes on to you—intensified!"

Mr. Reeder's idea of walking warily was peculiarly his own. He travelled down to Maidstone the next morning, and, finding a bus that passed the lodge gates of Elfreda Manor, he journeyed comfortably and economically, his umbrella between his knees. He passed through the lodge gates, up a long and winding avenue of poplars, and presently came within sight of the grey manor house.

In a deep chair on the lawn he saw a girl sitting, a book on her knees, and evidently she saw him, for she rose as he crossed the lawn and came toward him eagerly.

"I'm Miss Margaret Letherby—are you from——?" She mentioned the name of a well-known firm of lawyers, and her face fell when Mr. Reeder regretfully disclaimed connection with those legal lights.

She was as pretty as a perfect complexion and a round, not too intellectual, face could, in combination, make her.

"I thought—do you wish to see Sir James? He is in the library. If you ring, one of the maids will take you to him."

Had Mr. Reeder been the sort of man who could be puzzled by anything, he would have been puzzled by the suggestion that any girl with money of her own should marry a man much older than herself against her own wishes. There was little mystery in the matter now. Miss Margaret would have married any strong-willed man who insisted.

"Even me," said Mr. Reeder to himself, with a certain melancholy pleasure.

There was no need to ring the bell. A tall, broad man in a golfing suit stood in the doorway. His fair hair was long and hung over his forehead in a thick flat strand; a heavy tawny moustache hid his mouth and swept down over a chin that was long and powerful.

"Well?" he asked aggressively.

"I'm from the Public Prosecutor's office," murmured Mr. Reeder. "I have had an anonymous letter."

His pale eyes did not leave the face of the other man.

"Come in," said Sir James gruffly.

As he closed the door he glanced quickly first to the girl and then to the poplar avenue.

"I'm expecting a fool of a lawyer," he said, as he flung open the door of what was evidently the library.

His voice was steady; not by a flicker of eyelash had he betrayed the slightest degree of anxiety when Reeder had told his mission.

"Well—what about this anonymous letter? You don't take much notice of that kind of trash, do you?"

Mr. Reeder deposited his umbrella and flat-crowned hat on a chair before he took a document from his pocket and handed it to the baronet, who frowned as he read. Was it Mr. Reeder's vivid imagination, or did the hard light in the eyes of Sir James soften as he read?

"This is a cock and bull story of somebody having seen my wife's jewellery on sale in Paris," he said. "There is nothing in it. I can account for every one of my poor wife's trinkets. I brought back the jewel case after that awful night. I don't recognize the handwriting: who is the lying scoundrel who wrote this?"

Mr. Reeder had never before been called a lying scoundrel, but he accepted the experience with admirable meekness.

"I thought it untrue," he said, shaking his head. "I followed the details of the case very thoroughly. You left here in the afternoon——"

"At night," said the other brusquely. He was not inclined to discuss the matter, but Mr. Reeder's appealing look was irresistible. "It is only eighty minutes' run to Dover. We got to the pier at eleven o'clock, about the same time as the boat train, and we went on board at once. I got my cabin key from the purser and put her ladyship and her baggage inside."

"Her ladyship was a good sailor?"

"Yes, a very good sailor; she was remarkably well that night. I left her in the cabin dozing, and went for a stroll on the deck——"

"Raining very heavily and a strong sea running," nodded Reeder, as though in agreement with something the other man had said.

"Yes—I'm a pretty good sailor—anyway, that story about my poor wife's jewels is utter nonsense. You can tell the Director that, with my compliments."

He opened the door for his visitor, and Mr. Reeder was some time replacing the letter and gathering his belongings.

"You have a beautiful place here, Sir James—a lovely place. An extensive estate?"

"Three thousand acres." This time he did not attempt to disguise his impatience. "Good afternoon."

Mr. Reeder went slowly down the drive, his remarkable memory at work.

He missed the bus, which he could easily have caught, and pursued an apparently aimless way along the winding road which marched with the boundaries of the baronet's property. A walk of a quarter of a mile brought him to a lane shooting off at right angles from the main road, and marking, he guessed, the southern boundary. At the corner stood an old stone lodge, on the inside of a forbidding iron gate. The lodge was in a pitiable state of neglect and disrepair. Tiles had been dislodged from the roof, the windows were grimy or broken, and the little garden was overrun with docks and thistles. Beyond the gate was a narrow, weed-covered drive that trailed out of sight into a distant plantation.

Hearing the clang of a letter-box closing, he turned to see a postman mounting his bicycle.

"What place is this?" asked Mr. Reeder arresting the postman's departure.

"South Lodge—Sir James Tithermite's property. It's never used now. Hasn't been used for years—I don't know why; it's a short cut if they happen to be coming this way."

Mr. Reeder walked with him toward the village, and he was a skilful pumper of wells, however dry; and the postman was not dry by any means.

"Yes, poor lady! She was very frail—one of those sort of invalids that last out many a healthy man."

Mr. Reeder put a question at random and scored most unexpectedly.

"Yes, her ladyship was a bad sailor. I know because every time she went abroad she used to get a bottle of that stuff people take for seasickness. I've delivered many a bottle till Raikes, the chemist, stocked it—'Pickers' Travellers' Friend,' that's what it was called. Mr. Raikes was only saying to me the other day that he'd got half a dozen bottles on hand, and he didn't know what to do with them. Nobody in Climbury ever goes to sea."

Mr. Reeder went on to the village and idled his precious time in most unlikely places. At the chemist's, at the blacksmith shop, at the modest building yard. He caught the last bus back to Maidstone, and by great good luck the last train to London.

And, in his vague way, he answered the Director's query the next day with: "Yes, I saw Sir James: a very interesting man."

This was on the Friday. All day Saturday he was busy. The Sabbath brought him a new interest.

On this bright Sunday morning, Mr. Reeder, attired in a flowered dressing-gown, his feet encased in black velvet slippers, stood at the window of his house in Brockley Road and surveyed the deserted thoroughfare. The bell of a local church, which was accounted high, had rung for early Mass, and there was nothing living in sight except a black cat that lay asleep in a patch of sunlight on the top step of the house opposite. The hour was 7.30, and Mr. Reeder had been at his desk since six, working by artificial light, the month being October toward the close.

From the half-moon of the window bay he regarded a section of the Lewisham High Road and as much of Tanners Hill as can be seen before it dips past the railway bridge into sheer Deptford.

Returning to his table, he opened a carton of the cheapest cigarettes and, lighting one, puffed in an amateurish fashion. He smoked cigarettes rather like a woman who detests them but feels that it is the correct thing to do.

"Dear me," said Mr. Reeder feebly.

He was back at the window, and he had seen a man turn out of Lewisham High Road. He had crossed the road and was coming straight to

Daffodil House—which frolicsome name appeared on the door-posts of Mr. Reeder's residence. A tall, straight man, with a sombre brown face, he came to the front gate, passed through and beyond the watcher's range of vision.

"Dear me!" said Mr. Reeder, as he heard the tinkle of a bell.

A few minutes later his housekeeper tapped on the door.

"Will you see Mr. Kohl, sir?" she asked.

Mr. J. G. Reeder nodded.

Lew Kohl walked into the room to find a middle-aged man in a flamboyant dressing-gown sitting at his desk, a pair of pince-nez set crookedly on his nose.

"Good-morning, Kohl."

Lew Kohl looked at the man who had sent him to seven and a half years of hell, and the corners of his thin lips curled.

"'Morning, Mr. Reeder." His eyes flashed across the almost bare surface of the writing-desk on which Reeder's hands were lightly clasped. "You didn't expect to see me, I guess?"

"Not so early," said Reeder in his hushed voice, "but I should have remembered that early rising is one of the good habits which are inculcated by penal servitude."

He said this in the manner of one bestowing praise for good conduct.

"I suppose you've got a pretty good idea of why I have come, eh? I'm a bad forgetter, Reeder, and a man in Dartmoor has time to think."

The older man lifted his sandy eyebrows, the steel-rimmed glasses on his nose slipped further askew.

"That phrase seems familiar," he said, and the eyebrows lowered in a frown. "Now let me think—it was in a melodrama, of course, but was it 'Souls in Harness' or 'The Marriage Vow'?"

He appeared genuinely anxious for assistance in solving this problem.

"This is going to be a different kind of play," said the long-faced Lew through his teeth. "I'm going to get you, Reeder—you can go along and tell your boss, the Public Prosecutor. But I'll get you sweet! There will be no evidence to swing me. And I'll get that nice little stocking of yours, Reeder!"

The legend of Reeder's fortune was accepted by even so intelligent a man as Kohl.

"You'll get my stocking! Dear me, I shall have to go barefooted," said Mr. Reeder, with a faint show of humour.

"You know what I mean—think that over. Some hour and day you'll go out, and all Scotland Yard won't catch me for the killing! I've thought that out——"

"One has time to think in Dartmoor," murmured Mr. J. G. Reeder encouragingly. "You're becoming one of the world's thinkers, Kohl. Do you know Rodin's masterpiece—a beautiful statue throbbing with life——"

"That's all." Lew Kohl rose, the smile still trembling at the corner of his mouth. "Maybe you'll turn this over in your mind, and in a day or two you won't be feeling so gay."

Reeder's face was pathetic in its sadness. His untidy sandy-grey hair seemed to be standing on end; the large ears, that stood out at right angles to his face, gave the illusion of quivering movement.

Lew Kohl's hand was on the door-knob.

"Womp!"

It was the sound of a dull weight striking a board; something winged past his cheek, before his eyes a deep hole showed in the wall, and his face was stung by flying grains of plaster. He spun round with a whine of rage.

Mr. Reeder had a long-barrelled Browning in his hand, with a barrel-shaped silencer over the muzzle, and he was staring at the weapon open-mouthed.

"Now how on earth did that happen?" he asked in wonder.

Lew Kohl stood trembling with rage and fear, his face yellow-white.

"You—you swine!" he breathed. "You tried to shoot me!"

Mr. Reeder stared at him over his glasses.

"Good gracious—you think that? Still thinking of killing me, Kohl?"

Kohl tried to speak but found no words, and, flinging open the door, he strode down the stairs and through the front entrance. His foot was on the first step when something came hurtling past him and crashed to fragments at his feet. It was a large stone vase that had decorated the window-sill of Mr. Reeder's bedroom. Leaping over the débris of stone and flower mould, he glared up into the surprised face of Mr. J. G. Reeder.

"I'll get you!" he spluttered.

"I hope you're not hurt?" asked the man at the window in a tone of concern. "These things happen. Some day and some hour——"

As Lew Kohl strode down the street, the detective was still talking.

Mr. Stan Bride was at his morning ablutions when his friend and sometime prison associate came into the little room that overlooked Fitzroy Square.

Stan Bride, who bore no resemblance to anything virginal, being a stout and stumpy man with a huge red face and many chins, stopped in the act of drying himself and gazed over the edge of the towel.

"What's the matter with you?" he asked sharply. "You look as if you'd been chased by a busy. What did you go out so early for?"

Lew told him, and the jovial countenance of his roommate grew longer and longer.

"You poor fish!" he hissed. "To go after Reeder with that stuff! Don't you think he was waiting for you? Do you suppose he didn't know the very moment you left the Moor?"

"I've scared him, anyway," said the other, and Mr. Bride laughed.

"Good scout!" he sneered. "Scare that old person!" (He did not say "person.") "If he's as white as you, he *is* scared! But he's not. Of course he shot past you—if he'd wanted to shoot you, you'd have been stiff by now. But he didn't. Thinker, eh—he's given you somep'n' to think about."

"Where that gun came from I don't ——"

There was a knock at the door and the two men exchanged glances.

"Who's there?" asked Bride, and a familiar voice answered.

"It's that busy from the Yard," whispered Bride, and opened the door.

The "busy" was Sergeant Allford, C.I.D., an affable and portly man and a detective of some promise.

"'Morning, boys—not been to church, Stan?"

Stan grinned politely.

"How's trade, Lew?"

"Not so bad." The forger was alert, suspicious.

"Come to see you about a gun—got an idea you're carrying one, Lew— Colt automatic R.7/94318. That's not right, Lew—guns don't belong to this country."

"I've got no gun," said Lew sullenly.

Bride had suddenly become an old man, for he also was a convict on licence, and the discovery might send him back to serve his unfinished sentence.

"Will you come a little walk to the station, or will you let me go over you?"

"Go over me," said Lew, and put out his arms stiffly whilst the detective rubbed him down.

"I'll have a look round," said the detective, and his "look round" was very thorough.

"Must have been mistaken," said Sergeant Allford. And then, suddenly: "Was that what you chucked into the river as you were walking along the Embankment?"

Lew started. It was the first intimation he had received that he had been "tailed" that morning.

Bride waited till the detective was visible from the window crossing Fitzroy Square; then he turned in a fury on his companion.

"Clever, ain't you! That old hound knew you had a gun—knew the number. And if Allford had found it you'd have been 'dragged' and me too!"

"I threw it in the river," said Lew sulkily.

"Brains—not many but some!" said Bride, breathing heavily. "You cut out Reeder—he's hell and poison, and if you don't know it you're deaf! Scared him? You big stiff! He'd cut your throat and write a hymn about it."

"I didn't know they were tailing me," growled Kohl; "but I'll get him! And his money too."

"Get him from another lodging," said Bride curtly. "A crook I don't mind, being one; a murderer I don't mind, but a talking jackass makes me sick. Get his stuff if you can—I'll bet it's all invested in real estate, and you can't lift houses—but don't talk about it. I like you, Lew, up to a point; you're miles before the point and out of sight. I don't like Reeder—I don't like snakes, but I keep away from the Zoo."

So Lew Kohl went into new diggings on the top floor of an Italian's house in Dean Street, and here he had leisure and inclination to brood upon his grievances and to plan afresh the destruction of his enemy. And new plans were needed, for the schemes which had seemed so watertight in the quietude of a Devonshire cell showed daylight through many crevices.

Lew's homicidal urge had undergone considerable modification. He had been experimented upon by a very clever psychologist—though he never regarded Mr. Reeder in this light, and, indeed, had the vaguest idea as to what the word meant. But there were other ways of hurting Reeder, and his mind fell constantly back to the dream of discovering the peccant detective's hidden treasure.

It was nearly a week later that Mr. Reeder invited himself into the Director's private sanctum, and that great official listened spellbound while his subordinate offered his outrageous theory about Sir James Tithermite and his dead wife. When Mr. Reeder had finished, the Director pushed back his chair from the table.

"My dear man," he said, a little irritably, "I can't possibly give a warrant on the strength of your surmises—not even a search warrant. The story is so fantastic, so incredible, that it would be more at home in the pages of a sensational story than in a Public Prosecutor's report."

"It was a wild night, and yet Lady Tithermite was not ill," suggested the detective gently. "That is a fact to remember, sir."

The Director shook his head.

"I can't do it—not on the evidence," he said. "I should raise a storm that'd swing me into Whitehall. Can't you do anything—unofficially?"

Mr. Reeder shook his head.

"My presence in the neighbourhood has been remarked," he said primly. "I think it would be impossible to—er—cover up my traces. And yet I have located the place, and could tell you within a few inches——''

Again the Director shook his head.

"No, Reeder," he said quietly, "the whole thing is sheer deduction on your part. Oh, yes, I know you have a criminal mind—I think you have told me that before. And that is a good reason why I should not issue a warrant. You're simply crediting this unfortunate man with your ingenuity. Nothing doing!''

Mr. Reeder sighed and went back to his bureau, not entirely despondent, for there had intruded a new element into his investigations.

Mr. Reeder had been to Maidstone several times during the week, and he had not gone alone; though seemingly unconscious of the fact that he had developed a shadow, for he had seen Lew Kohl on several occasions, and had spent an uncomfortable few minutes wondering whether his experiment had failed.

On the second occasion an idea had developed in the detective's mind, and if he were a laughing man he would have chuckled aloud when he slipped out of Maidstone station one evening and, in the act of hiring a cab, had seen Lew Kohl negotiating for another.

Mr. Bride was engaged in the tedious but necessary practice of so cutting a pack of cards that the ace of diamonds remained at the bottom, when his former co-lodger burst in upon him, and there was a light of triumph in Lew's cold eye which brought Mr. Bride's heart to his boots.

"I've got him!" said Lew.

Bride put aside the cards and stood up.

"Got who?" he asked coldly. "And if it's killing, you needn't answer, but get out!''

"There's no killing.''

Lew sat down squarely at the table, his hands in his pockets, a real smile on his face.

"I've been trailing Reeder for a week, and that fellow wants some trailing!''

"Well?" asked the other, when he paused dramatically.

"I've found his stocking!''

Bride scratched his chin, and was half convinced.

"You have?''

Lew nodded.

"He's been going to Maidstone a lot lately, and driving to a little village about five miles out. There I always lost him. But the other night, when he came back to the station to catch the last train, he slipped into the waiting room and I found a place where I could watch him. What do you think he did?''

Mr. Bride hazarded no suggestion.

"He opened his bag," said Lew impressively, "and took out a wad of notes as thick as that! He'd been drawing on his bank! I trailed him up to London. There's a restaurant on the station and he went in to get a cup of coffee, with me keeping well out of his sight. As he came out of the restaurant he took out his handkerchief and wiped his mouth. He didn't see the little book that dropped, but I did. I was scared sick that somebody else would see it, or that he'd wait long enough to find it himself. But he went out of the station and I got that book before you could say 'knife.' Look!"

It was a well-worn little notebook, covered with faded red morocco. Bride put out his hand to take it.

"Wait a bit," said Lew. "Are you in this with me fifty-fifty, because I want some help."

Bride hesitated.

"If it's just plain thieving, I'm with you," he said.

"Plain thieving—and sweet," said Lew exultantly, and pushed the book across the table.

For the greater part of the night they sat together talking in low tones, discussing impartially the methodical bookkeeping of Mr. J. G. Reeder and his exceeding dishonesty.

The Monday night was wet. A storm blew up from the southwest, and the air was filled with falling leaves as Lew and his companion footed the five miles which separated them from the village. Neither carried any impedimenta that was visible, yet under Lew's waterproof coat was a kit of tools of singular ingenuity, and Mr. Bride's coat pockets were weighted down with the sections of a powerful jemmy.

They met nobody in their walk, and the church bell was striking eleven when Lew gripped the bars of the South Lodge gates, pulled himself up to the top and dropped lightly on the other side. He was followed by Mr. Bride, who, in spite of his bulk, was a singularly agile man. The ruined lodge showed in the darkness, and they passed through the creaking gates to the door and Lew flashed his lantern upon the keyhole before he began manipulation with the implements which he had taken from his kit.

The door was opened in ten minutes and a few seconds later they stood in a low-roofed little room, the principal feature of which was a deep, grateless fireplace. Lew took off his mackintosh and stretched it over the window before he spread the light in his lamp, and, kneeling down, brushed the débris from the hearth, examining the joints of the big stone carefully.

"This work's been botched," he said. "Anybody could see that."

He put the claw of the jemmy into a crack and levered up the stone, and it moved slightly. Stopping only to dig a deeper crevice with a chisel and hammer he thrust the claw of the jemmy farther down. The stone came up above the edge of the floor and Bride slipped the chisel underneath.

"Now together," grunted Lew.

They got their fingers beneath the hearthstone and with one heave hinged it up. Lew picked up the lamp and, kneeling down, flashed a light into the dark cavity. And then:

"Oh, my God!" he shrieked.

A second later two terrified men rushed from the house into the drive. And a miracle had happened, for the gates were open and a dark figure stood squarely before them.

"Put up your hands, Kohl!" said a voice, and, hateful as it was to Lew Kohl, he could have fallen on the neck of Mr. Reeder.

At twelve o'clock that night Sir James Tithermite was discussing matters with his bride-to-be: the stupidity of her lawyer, who wished to safeguard her fortune, and his own cleverness and foresight in securing complete freedom of action for the girl who was to be his wife.

"These blackguards think of nothing but their fees," he began, when his footman came in unannounced, and behind him the Chief Constable of the county and a man he remembered seeing before.

"Sir James Tithermite?" said the Chief Constable unnecessarily, for he knew Sir James very well.

"Yes, Colonel, what is it?" asked the baronet, his face twitching.

"I am taking you into custody on a charge of wilfully murdering your wife, Eleanor Mary Tithermite."

* * * * *

"The whole thing turned upon the question as to whether Lady Tithermite was a good or a bad sailor," explained J. G. Reeder to his chief. "If she were a bad sailor, it was unlikely that she would be on the ship, even for five minutes, without calling for the stewardess. The stewardess did not see her ladyship, nor did anybody on board, for the simple reason that she was not on board! She was murdered within the grounds of the Manor; her body was buried beneath the hearthstone of the old lodge, and Sir James continued his journey by car to Dover, handing over his packages to a porter and telling him to take them to his cabin before he returned to put the car into the hotel garage. He had timed his arrival so that he passed on board with a crowd of passengers from the boat train, and nobody knew whether he was alone or whether he was accompanied, and, for the matter of that, nobody cared. The purser gave him his key, and he put the baggage, including his wife's hat, into the cabin, paid the porter and dismissed him. Officially, Lady Tithermite was on board, for he surrendered her ticket to the collector and received her landing voucher. And then he discovered she had disappeared. The ship was searched, but of course the unfortunate lady was not found. As I remarked before——"

"You have a criminal mind," said the Director good-humouredly. "Go on, Reeder."

"Having this queer and objectionable trait, I saw how very simple a matter it was to give the illusion that the lady was on board, and I decided that, if the murder was committed, it must have been within a few miles of the house. And then the local builder told me that he had given Sir James a little lesson in the art of mixing mortar. And the local blacksmith told me that the gate had been damaged, presumably by Sir James's car—I had seen the broken rods and all I wanted to know was when the repairs were effected. That she was beneath the hearth in the lodge I was certain. Without a search warrant it was impossible to prove or disprove my theory, and I myself could not conduct a private investigation without risking the reputation of our department—if I may say 'our'," he said apologetically.

The Director was thoughtful.

"Of course, you induced this man Kohl to dig up the hearth by pretending you had money buried there. I presume you revealed that fact in your notebook? But why on earth did he imagine that you had a hidden treasure?"

Mr. Reeder smiled sadly.

"The criminal mind is a peculiar thing," he said, with a sigh. "It harbours illusions and fairy stories. Fortunately, I understand that mind. As I have often said . . ."

III

The Troupe

There was a quietude and sedateness about the Public Prosecutor's office which completely harmonised with the tastes and inclinations of Mr. J. G. Reeder. For he was a gentleman who liked to work in an office where the ticking of a clock was audible and the turning of a paper produced a gentle disturbance.

He had before him one morning the typewritten catalogue of Messrs. Willoby, the eminent estate agents, and he was turning the leaves with a thoughtful expression. The catalogue was newly arrived, a messenger having only a few minutes before placed the portfolio on his desk.

Presently he smoothed down a leaf and read again the flattering description of a fairly unimportant property, and his scrutiny was patently a waste of time, for, scrawled on the margin of the sheet in red ink was the word "Let," which meant that "Riverside Bower" was not available for hire. The ink was smudged, and "Let" had been obviously written that morning.

"Humph!" said Mr. Reeder.

He was interested for many reasons. In the heat of July riverside houses are at a premium: at the beginning of November they are somewhat of a drug on the market. And transatlantic visitors do not as a rule hire riverside cottages in a month which is chiefly distinguished by mists, rain, and general discomfort.

Two reception; two bedrooms; bath, large dry cellars, lawn to river, small skiff and punt. Gas and electric light. Three guineas weekly or would be let for six months at 2 guineas.

He pulled his table telephone toward him and gave the agents' number.

"Let, is it—dear me! To an American gentleman? When will it be available?"

The new tenant had taken the house for a month. Mr. Reeder was even more intrigued, though his interest in the "American gentleman" was not quite as intensive as the American gentleman's interest in Mr. Reeder.

When the great Art Lomer came on a business trip from Canada to Lon-

don, a friend and admirer carried him off one day to see the principal sight
of London.

"He generally comes out at lunch time," said the friend, who was called
"Cheep," because his name was Sparrow.

Mr. Lomer looked up and down Whitehall disparagingly, for he had
seen so many cities of the world that none seemed as good as the others.

"There he is!" whispered Cheep, though there was no need for mystery
or confidence.

A middle-aged man had come out of one of the narrow doorways of a
large grey building. On his head was a high, flat-crowned hat, his body was
tightly encased in a black frock-coat. A weakish man with yellowy-white
side whiskers and eyeglasses that were nearer to the end than the beginning
of his nose.

"Him?" demanded the amazed Art.

"Him," said the other, incorrectly but with emphasis.

"Is that the kind of guy you're scared about? You're crazy. Why, that
man couldn't catch a cold! Now, back home in T'ronto——"

Art was proud of his home town, and in that spirit of expansiveness
which paints even the unpleasant features of One's Own with the most attractive hues, he had even a good word to say about the Royal Canadian
Police—a force which normally, and in a local atmosphere, he held in the
greatest detestation.

Art "operated"—he never employed a baser word—from Toronto,
which, by its proximity to Buffalo and the United States border, gave him
certain advantages. He had once "operated" in Canada itself, but his line
at that period being robbery of a kind which is necessarily accompanied by
assault, he had found himself facing a Canadian magistrate, and a Canadian magistrate wields extraordinary powers. Art had been sent down for
five years and, crowning horror, was ordered to receive twenty-five lashes
with a whip which has nine tails, each one of which hurts. Thereafter he cut
out violence and confined himself to the formation of his troupe—and Art
Lomer's troupe was famous from the Atlantic to the Pacific.

He had been plain Arthur Lomer when he was rescued from a London
gutter and a career of crime and sent to Canada, the charitable authorities
being under the impression that Canada was rather short on juvenile
criminals. By dint of great artfulness, good stage management, and a
natural aptitude for acquiring easy money, he had gained for himself a
bungalow on the islands, a flat in Church Street, a six-cylinder car, and a
New England accent which would pass muster in almost any place except
New England.

"I'll tell the world you fellows want waking up! So that's your Reeder?

Well, if Canada and the United States was full of goats like him, I'd pack more dollars in one month than Hollywood pays Chaplin in ten years. Yes, sir. Listen, does that guy park a clock?''

His guide was a little dazed.

"Does he wear a watch? Sure!"

Mr. Art Lomer nodded.

"Wait—I'll bring it back to you in five minutes—I'm goin' to show you sump'n'.''

It was the maddest fool thing he had ever done in his life; he was in London on business, and was jeopardising a million dollars for the sake of the cheap applause of a man for whose opinion he did not care a cent.

Mr. Reeder was standing nervously on the sidewalk, waiting for what he described as "the vehicular traffic" to pass, when a strange man bumped against him.

"Excuse me, sir," said the stranger.

"Not at all," murmured Mr. Reeder. "My watch is five minutes fast—you can see the correct time by Big Ben."

Mr. Lomer felt a hand dip into his coat pocket, saw, like one hypnotised, the watch go back to J. G. Reeder's pocket.

"Over here for long?" asked Mr. Reeder pleasantly.

"Why—yes."

"It's a nice time of the year." Mr. Reeder removed his eyeglasses, rubbed them feebly on his sleeve and replaced them crookedly. "But the country is not quite so beautiful as Canada in the fall. How is Leoni?"

Art Lomer did not faint; he swayed slightly and blinked hard, as if he were trying to wake up. Leoni was the proprietor of that little restaurant in Buffalo which was the advanced base of those operations so profitable to Art and his friends.

"Leoni? Say, mister——"

"And the troupe—are they performing in England or—er—resting? I think that is the word."

Art gaped at the other. On Mr. Reeder's face was an expression of solicitude and enquiry. It was as though the well-being of the troupe was an absorbing preoccupation.

"Say—listen——" began Art huskily.

Before he could collect his thoughts Reeder was crossing the road with nervous glances left and right, his umbrella gripped tightly in his hand.

"I guess I'm crazy," said Mr. Lomer, and walked back very slowly to where he had left his anxious cicerone.

"No—he got away before I could touch him," he said briefly, for he had his pride. "Come along, we'll get some eats, it's nearly twel——"

He put his hand to his pocket, but his watch was gone! So also was the expensive platinum albert. Mr. Reeder could be heavily jocular on occasions.

"Art Lomer—is there anything against him?" asked the Director of Public Prosecutions, whose servant Mr. J. G. Reeder was.

"No, sir, there is no complaint here. I have come into—er—possession of a watch of his, which I find, by reference to my private file, was stolen in Cleveland in 1921—it is in the police file of that date. Only—um—it seems remarkable that this gentleman should be in London at the end of the tourist season."

The Director pursed his lips dubiously.

"M—m. Tell the people at the Yard. He doesn't belong to us. What is his specialty?"

"He is a troupe leader—I think that is the term. Mr. Lomer was once associated with a theatrical company in—er—a humble capacity."

"You mean he is an actor?" asked the puzzled Director.

"Ye-es, sir; a producer rather than actor. I have heard about his troupe, though I have never had the pleasure of seeing them perform. A talented company."

He sighed heavily and shook his head.

"I don't quite follow you about the troupe. How did his watch come into your possession, Reeder?"

"That was a little jest on my part," he said, lowering his voice. "A little jest."

The Director knew Mr. Reeder too well to pursue the subject.

Lomer was living at the Hotel Calfort, in Bloomsbury. He occupied an important suite, for, being in the position of a man who was after big fish, he could not cavil at the cost of the groundbait. The big fish had bitten much sooner than Art Lomer had dared to hope. Its name was Bertie Claude Staffen, and the illustration was apt, for there was something very fishlike about this young man with his dull eyes and his permanently opened mouth.

Bertie's father was rich beyond the dreams of actresses. He was a pottery manufacturer, who bought cotton mills as a side-line, and he had made so much money that he never hired a taxi if he could take a bus, and never took a bus if he could walk. In this way he kept his liver (to which he frequently referred) in good order and hastened the degeneration of his heart.

Bertie Claude had inherited all his father's meanness and such of his money as was not left to faithful servants, orphan homes and societies for promoting the humanities, which meant that Bertie inherited almost every penny. He had the weak chin and sloping forehead of an undeveloped intellect, but he knew there were twelve pennies to a shilling and that one hundred cents equalled one dollar, and that is more knowledge than the only sons of millionaires usually acquire.

He had one quality which few would suspect in him: the gift of romantic dreaming. When Mr. Staffen was not occupied in cutting down overhead charges or speeding up production, he loved to sit at his ease, a cigarette between his lips, his eyes half closed, and picture himself in heroic situations. Thus, he would imagine dark caves stumbled upon by accident, filled with dusty boxes bulging with treasure; or he saw himself at Deauville Casino, with immense piles of *mille* notes before him, won from fabulously rich Greeks, Armenians—in fact, anybody who is fabulously rich. Most of his dreams were about money in sufficient quantities to repay him for the death duties on his father's estate which had been iniquitously wrung from him by thieving revenue officers. He was a very rich man, but ought to be richer—this was his considered view.

When Bertie Claude arrived at the Calfort Hotel and was shown into Art's private sitting-room, he stepped into a world of heady romance. For the big table in the centre of the room was covered with specimens of quartz of every grade, and they had been recovered from a brand-new mine located by Art's mythical brother and sited at a spot which was known only to two men, one of whom was Art Lomer and the other Bertie Claude Staffen.

Mr. Staffen took off his light overcoat and, walking to the table, inspected the ore with sober interest.

"I've had the assay," he said. "The johnny who did it is a friend of mine and didn't charge a penny; his report is promising—very promising."

"The company——" began Art, but Mr. Staffen raised a warning finger.

"I think you know, and it is unnecessary for me to remind you, that I do not intend speculating a dollar in this mine. I'm putting up no money. What I'm prepared to do is to use my influence in the promotion for a *quid pro quo*. You know what that means?"

"Something for nothing!" said Art, and in this instance was not entirely wide of the mark.

"Well, no—stock in the company. Maybe I'll take a directorship later, when the money is up and everything is plain sailing. I can't lend my name to a—well, unknown quantity."

Art agreed.

"My friend has put up the money," he said easily. "If that guy had another hundred dollars he'd have all the money in the world—he's that rich. Stands to reason, Mr. Staffen, that I wouldn't come over here tryin' to get money from a gentleman who is practically a stranger. We met in

Canada—sure we did! But what do you know about me? I might be one large crook—I might be a con man or anything!"

Some such idea had occurred to Bertie Claude, but the very frankness of his friend dispelled something of his suspicions.

"I've often wondered since what you must have thought of me, sittin' in a game with that bunch of thugs," Art went on, puffing a reflective cigar. "But I guess you said to yourself, 'This guy is a man of the world—he's *gotta* mix.' An' that's true. In these Canadian mining camps you horn in with some real tough boys—yes, sir. They're sump'n' fierce."

"I quite understood the position," said Bertie Claude, who hadn't. "I flatter myself I know men. If I haven't shown that in 'Homo Sum' then I've failed in expression."

"Sure," said Mr. Lomer lazily, and added another "Sure!" to ram home the first. "That's a pretty good book. When you give it to me at King Edward Hotel I thought it was sump'n' about arithmetic. But it's mighty good poetry, every line startin' with big letters an' the end of every line sounding like the end word in the line before. I said to my secretary, 'That Mr. Staffen must have a brain.' How you get the ideas beats me. That one about the princess who comes out of a clam——"

"An oyster—she was the embodiment of the pearl," Bertie hastened to explain. "You mean 'The White Maiden'?"

Lomer nodded lazily.

"That was grand. I never read poetry till I read that; it just made me want to cry like a great big fool! If I had your gifts I wouldn't be loafin' round Ontario prospecting. No, sir."

"It *is* a gift," said Mr. Staffen after thought. "You say you have the money for the company?"

"Every cent. I'm not in a position to offer a single share—that's true. Not that you need worry about that. I've reserved a few from promotion. No, sir, I never had any intention of allowing you to pay a cent."

He knocked off the ash of his cigar and frowned.

"You've been mighty nice to me, Mr. Staffen," he said slowly, "and though I don't feel called upon to tell every man my business, you're such a square white fellow that I feel sort of confident about you. This mine means nothing."

Bertie Claude's eyebrows rose.

"I don't quite get you," he said.

Art's smile was slow and a little sad.

"Doesn't it occur to you that if I've got the capital for that property, it was foolish of me to take a trip to Europe?"

Bertie had certainly wondered why.

"Selling that mine was like selling bars of gold. It didn't want any doing; I could have sold it if I'd been living in the Amaganni Forest. No, sir, I'm here on business that would make your hair stand up if you knew."

He rose abruptly and paced the room with quick, nervous strides, his brow furrowed in thought.

"You're a whale of a poet," he said suddenly. "Maybe you've got more imagination than most people. What does the mine mean for me? A few hundred thousand dollars' profit." He shrugged his shoulders. "What are you doing on Wednesday?"

The brusqueness of the question took Bertie Claude aback.

"On Wednesday? Well, I don't know that I'm doing anything."

Mr. Lomer bit his lip thoughtfully.

"I've got a little house on the river. Come down and spend a night with me, and I'll let you into a secret that these newspapers would give a million dollars to know. If you read it in a book you wouldn't believe it. Maybe one day you can write it. It would take a man with your imagination to put it over. Say, I'll tell you now."

And then, with some hesitation, Mr. Lomer told his story.

"Politics, and all that, I know nothing about. But ever since the revolution in Russia, queer things have been happenin'. I'm not such a dunce that I don't know that. My interest in Russia was about the same as yours in Piketown, Saskatchewan. But about six months ago I got in touch with a couple of Russkis. They came out of the United States in a hurry, with a sheriff's posse behind them, and I happened to be staying on a farm near the border when they turned up. And what do you think they'd been doing?"

Mr. Staffen shook his head.

"Peddling emeralds," said the other soberly.

"Emeralds? Peddling? What do you mean—trying to sell emeralds?"

Art nodded.

"Yes, sir. One had a paper bag full of 'em, all sizes. I bought the lot for twelve thousand dollars, took 'em down to T'ronto and got them valued at something under a million dollars."

Bertie Claude was listening open-mouthed.

"These fellows had come from Moscow. They'd been peddlin' jewellery for four years. Some broken-down Prince was acting as agent for the other swells—I didn't ask questions too closely, because naturally I'm not inquisitive."

He leaned forward and tapped the other's knee to emphasise his words.

"The stuff I bought wasn't a twentieth of their stock. I sent them back to Russia for the rest of the loot, and they're due here next week."

"Twenty million dollars!" gasped Bertie Claude. "What will it cost you?"

"A million dollars—two hundred thousand pounds. Come down to my place at Marlow, and I'll show you the grandest emeralds you ever saw—all that I've got left, as a matter of fact. I sold the biggest part to a Pittsburg millionaire for—well, I won't give you the price, because you'll think I robbed him! If you like any stone you see—why, I'll let you buy it, though I don't want to sell. Naturally, I couldn't make profit out of a friend."

Bertie Claude listened, dazed, while his host catalogued his treasures with an ease and a shrewd sense of appraisement. When Mr. Staffen left his friend's room, his head was in a whirl, though he experienced a bewildered sense of familiarity with a situation which had often figured in his dreams.

As he strode through the hall, he saw a middle-aged man with a flat-topped felt hat, but beyond noticing that he wore a ready-made cravat, that his shoes were square-toed and that he looked rather like a bailiff's officer, Bertie Claude would have passed him, had not the old-fashioned gentleman stood in his way.

"Excuse me, sir. You're Mr. Staffen, are you not?"

"Yes," said Bertie shortly.

"I wonder if I could have a few moments' conversation with you on—er —a matter of some moment?"

Bertie waved an impatient hand.

"I've no time to see anybody," he said brusquely. "If you want an appointment you'd better write for it."

And he walked out, leaving the sad-looking man to gaze pensively after him.

Mr. Lomer's little house was an isolated stone bungalow between Marlow and the Quarry Wood, and if he had sought diligently, Mr. Lomer could not have found a property more suitable for his purpose. Bertie Claude, who associated the river with sunshine and flannelled ease, shivered as he came out of the railway station and looked anxiously up at the grey sky. It was raining steadily, and the station cab that was waiting for him dripped from every surface.

"Pretty beastly month to take a bungalow on the river," he grumbled.

Mr. Lomer, who was not quite certain in his mind what was the ideal month for riverside bungalows, agreed.

"It suits me," he said. "This house of mine has got the right kind of lonesomeness. I just hate having people looking over me."

The road from the station to the house followed parallel with the line of the river. Staring out of the streaming windows, Mr. Staffen saw only the steel-grey of water and the damp grasses of the meadows through which the road ran. A quarter of an hour's drive, however, brought them to a pretty little cottage which stood in a generous garden. A bright fire burnt in the hall fireplace and there was a general air of cosiness and comfort about the place that revived Bertie's flagging spirits. A few seconds later they were sitting in a half-timbered dining-room, where tea had been laid.

Atmosphere has an insensible appeal to most people, and Bertie found himself impressed alike by the snugness of the place and the unexpected service, for there were a trim, pretty waiting maid, a sedate, middle-aged butler, and a sober-faced young man in footman's livery, who had taken off his wet mackintosh and had rubbed his boots dry before he entered the dining-room.

"No, the house isn't mine: it is one I always hire when I'm in England," said Mr. Lomer, who never told a small and unnecessary lie; because small and unnecessary lies are so easily detected. "Jenkins, the butler, is my man, so is the valet; the other people I just hired with the house."

After tea he showed Bertie up to his bedroom, and, opening a drawer of his bureau, took out a small steel box, fastened with two locks. These he unfastened and lifted out a shallow metal tray covered with a layer of cotton-wool.

"You can have any of these that take your eye," he said. "Make me an offer and I'll tell you what they're worth."

He rolled back the cottonwool and revealed six magnificent stones.

"That one?" said Mr. Lomer, taking the largest between his finger and thumb. "Why that's worth six thousand dollars—about twelve hundred pounds. And if you offered me that sum for it, I'd think you were a fool, because the only safe way of getting emeralds is to buy 'em fifty per cent. under value. I reckon that cost me about"—he made a mental calculation—"ninety pounds."

Bertie's eyes shone. On emeralds he was something of an expert, and that these stones were genuine, he knew.

"You wouldn't like to sell it for ninety pounds?" he asked carelessly.

Art Lomer shook his head.

"No, sir. I've gotta make some profit even from my friends! I'll let you have it for a hundred."

Bertie's hand sought his inside pocket.

"No, I don't want paying now. What do you know about emeralds anyway? They might be a clever fake. Take it up to town, show it to an expert——"

"I'll give you the check now."

"Any time will do."

Art wrapped up the stone carefully, put it in a small box and handed it to his companion.

"That's the only one I'm going to sell," he explained as he led the way back to the dining-room.

Bertie went immediately to the small secretaire, wrote the check and handed it to Mr. Lomer. Art looked at the paper and frowned.

"Why, what do I do with this?" he asked. "I've got no bank account here. All my money's in the Associated Express Company."

"I'll make it 'pay bearer,' " said Bertie obligingly.

Still Mr. Lomer was dubious.

"Just write a note telling the President, or whoever he is, to cash that little bit of paper. I hate banks anyway."

The obliging Bertie Claude scribbled the necessary note. When that was done, Bertie came to business, for he was a business man.

"Can I come in on this jewel deal?"

Art Lomer shook his head reluctantly.

"Sorry, Mr. Staffen, but that's almost impossible. I'll be quite frank with you, because I believe in straightforward dealing. When you ask to come in on that transaction, you're just asking me for money!"

Bertie made a faint noise of protest.

"Well, that's a mean way of putting it, but it comes to the same thing. I've taken all the risk, I've organised the operation—and it's cost money to get that guy out of Russia: aëroplanes and special trains and everything. I just hate to refuse you, because I like you, Mr. Staffen. Maybe if there's any little piece to which you might take a fancy, I'll let you have it at a reasonable price."

Bertie thought for a moment, his busy mind at work.

"What has the deal cost you up to now?" he asked.

Again Mr. Lomer shook his head.

"It doesn't matter what it's cost me—if you offered me four times the amount of money I've spent—and that would be a considerable sum—I couldn't let you in on this deal. I might go so far as giving you a small interest, but I wouldn't take money for that."

"We'll talk about it later," said Bertie, who never lost hope.

The rain had ceased, and the setting sun flooded the river with pale gold, and Bertie was walking in the garden with his host, when from somewhere above them came the faint hum of an aëroplane engine. Presently he saw the machine circling and disappearing behind the black crown of Quarry Wood. He heard an exclamation from the man at his side and, turning, saw Art's face puckered in a grimace of annoyance and doubt.

"What's the matter?" he asked.

"I'm wondering," said Art slowly. "They told me next week . . . why, no, I'm foolish."

It was dark. The butler had turned on the lights and drawn the blinds when they went indoors again, and it was not difficult for Bertie to realise that something had happened which was very disturbing to his host. He was taciturn, and for the next half-hour scarcely spoke, sitting in front of the fire gazing into the leaping flames and starting at every sound.

Dinner, a simple meal, was served early; and while the servants were clearing away, the two men strolled into the tiny drawing-room.

"What's the trouble, Lomer?"

"Nothing," said the other with a start, "only——"

At that moment they heard the tinkle of a bell, and Art listened tensely. He heard the parley of voices in the hall, and then the footman came.

"There's two men and a lady to see you, sir," he said.

Bertie saw the other bite his lip.

"Show them in," said Art curtly, and a second later a tall man, wearing the leather coat and helmet of an airman, walked into the room.

"Marsham! What in hell——!"

The girl who followed instantly claimed Bertie Claude's attention. She was slim and dark, and her face was beautiful despite the pallor of her cheeks and the tired look in her eyes. The second of the men visitors was hardly as prepossessing: a squat, foreign-looking individual with a short-clipped beard, he was wrapped to his neck in an old fur overcoat, and his wild-looking head was bare.

Art closed the door.

"What's the great idea?" he asked.

"There's been trouble," said the tall man sulkily. "The Prince has had another offer. He has sent some of the stuff, but he won't part with the pearls or the diamonds until you pay him half of the money you promised. This is Princess Pauline Dimitroff, the Prince's daughter," he explained.

Art shot an angry look at the girl.

"Say, see here, young lady," he said, "I suppose you speak English?"

She nodded.

"This isn't the way we do business in our country. Your father promised
——"

"My father has been very precipitate," she said, with the slightest of foreign accent, which was delightful to Bertie's ear. "He has taken much risk. Indeed, I am not sure that he has been very honest in the matter. It is very simple for you to pay. If he has your money to-night——"

"To-night?" boomed Art. "How can I get the money for him to-night?"

"He is in Holland," said the girl. "We have the aëroplane waiting."

"But how can I get the money to-night?" repeated the Canadian angrily. "Do you think I carry a hundred thousand pounds in my pistol pocket?"

Again she shrugged, and, turning to the unkempt little man, said something to him in a language which was unintelligible to Mr. Staffen. He replied in his hoarse voice, and she nodded.

"Pieter says my father will take your check. He only wishes to be sure that there is no——" She paused, at a loss for an English word.

"Did I ever double-cross your father?" asked Art savagely. "I can't give you either the money or the check. You can call off the deal—I'm through!"

By this time the aviator had unrolled the package he carried under his arm, placed it on the table, and Bertie Claude grew breathless at the sight of the glittering display that met his eyes. There were diamonds, set and unset; quaint and ancient pieces of jewellery that must have formed the heirlooms of old families; but their historical value did not for the moment occur to him. He beckoned Art aside.

"If you can keep these people here to-night," he said in a low voice, "I'll undertake to raise all the money you want on that collection alone."

Art shook his head.

"It's no use, Mr. Staffen. I know this guy. Unless I can send him the money to-night, we'll not smell the rest of the stuff."

Suddenly he clapped his hands.

"Gee!" he breathed. "That's an idea! You've got your check-book."

Cold suspicion showed in the eyes of Bertie Claude.

"I've got my check-book, certainly," he said, "but——"

"Come into the dining-room." Art almost ran ahead of him, and when they reached the room he closed the door. "A check can't be presented for two or three days. It certainly couldn't be presented to-morrow," he said, speaking rapidly. "By that time we could get this stuff up to town to your bankers, and you could keep it until I redeem it. What's more, you can stop payment of the check to-morrow morning if the stones aren't worth the money."

Bertie looked at the matter from ten different angles in as many seconds.

"Suppose I gave them a post-dated check to make sure?" he said.

"Post-dated?" Mr. Lomer was puzzled. "What does that mean?" And when Bertie explained, his face brightened. "Why, sure!" he said. "That's a double protection. Make it payable the day after to-morrow."

Bertie hesitated no more. Sitting down at the table he took out his check-book and a fountain pen, and verified the date.

"Make it 'bearer,' " suggested Art, when the writer paused, "same as you did the other check."

Bertie nodded and added his signature, with its characteristic under-lining.

"Wait a second."

Art went out of the room and came back within a minute.

"They've taken it!" he said exultantly. "Boy," he said, as he slapped the gratified young man on the shoulder, "you've gotta come in on this now and I didn't want you to. It's fifty-fifty—I'm no hog. Come along, and I'll show you something else that I never intended showing a soul."

He went out into the passage, opened a little door that led down a flight of stone steps to the cellar, switching on the light as he went down the stairs. Unlocking a heavy door, he threw it open.

"See here," he said, "did you ever see anything like this?"

Bertie Claude peered into the dark interior.

"I don't see——" he began, when he was so violently pushed into the darkness that he stumbled.

In another second the door closed on him; he heard the snap of a lock and shrieked:

"I say, what's this!"

"I say, you'll find out in a day or two," said the mocking voice of Mr. Lomer.

Art closed the second door, ran lightly up the stairs and joined the footman, butler, trim maid, and the three visitors in the drawing-room.

"He's well inside. And he stays there till the check matures—there's enough food and water in the cellar to last him a week."

"Did you get him?" asked the bearded Russian.

"Get him! He was easy," said the other scornfully. "Now, you boys and girls, skip, and skip quick! I've got a letter from this guy to his bank manager, telling him to——" he consulted the letter and quoted—" 'to cash the attached check for my friend Mr. Arthur Lomer.' "

There was a murmur of approval from the troupe.

"The aëroplane's gone back, I suppose?"

The man in the leather coat nodded.

"Yes," he said, "I only hired it for this afternoon."

"Well, you can get back too. Ray and Al, you go to Paris and take the C.P. boat from Havre. Slicky, you get those whiskers off and leave honest from Liverpool. Pauline and Aggie will make Genoa, and we'll meet at Leoni's on the fourteenth of next month and cut the stuff all ways!"

* * * * *

Two days later Mr. Art Lomer walked into the noble offices of the Northern Commercial Bank and sought an interview with the manager. That gentleman read the letter, examined the check and touched a bell.

"It's a mighty big sum," said Mr. Lomer, in an almost awe-stricken voice.

The manager smiled.

"We cash fairly large checks here," he said, and, to the clerk who came at his summons: "Mr. Lomer would like as much of this in American currency as possible. How did you leave Mr. Staffen?"

"Why, Bertie and I have been in Paris over that new company of mine," said Lomer. "My! it's difficult to finance Canadian industries in this country, Mr. Soames, but we've made a mighty fine deal in Paris."

He chatted on purely commercial topics until the clerk returned and laid a heap of bills and bank-notes on the table. Mr. Lomer produced a wallet, enclosed the money securely, shook hands with the manager, and walked out into the general office. And then he stopped, for Mr. J. G. Reeder stood squarely in his path.

"Pay-day for the troupe, Mr. Lomer—or do you call it 'treasury'? My theatrical glossary is rather rusty."

"Why, Mr. Reeder," stammered Art, "glad to see you, but I'm rather busy just now——"

"What do you think has happened to our dear friend, Mr. Bertie Claude Staffen?" asked Reeder anxiously.

"Why, he's in Paris."

"So soon!" murmured Reeder. "And the police only took him out of your suburban cellar an hour ago! How wonderful are our modern systems of transportation! Marlow one minute, Paris the next, and Moscow, let us say, the next."

Art hesitated no longer. He dashed past, thrusting the detective aside, and flew for the door. He was so annoyed that the two men who were waiting for him had the greatest difficulty in putting the handcuffs on his wrists.

*　　*　　*　　*　　*

"Yes, sir," said Mr. Reeder to his chief, "Art always travels with his troupe. The invisibility of the troupe was to me a matter for grave suspicion, and of course I've had the house under observation ever since Mr. Staffen disappeared. It is not my business, of course," he said apologetically, "and really I should not have interfered. Only, as I have often explained to you, the curious workings of my mind . . ."

IV

The Stealer of Marble

Margaret Belman's chiefest claim to Mr. Reeder's notice was that she lived in the Brockley Road, some few doors from his own establishment. He did not know her name, being wholly incurious about law-abiding folk, but he was aware that she was pretty, that her complexion was that pink and white which is seldom seen away from a magazine cover. She dressed well, and if there was one thing that he noted about her more than any other, it was that she walked and carried herself with a certain grace that was especially pleasing to a man of æsthetic predilections.

He had, on occasions, walked behind her and before her, and had ridden on the same street car with her to Westminster Bridge. She invariably descended at the corner of the Embankment, and was as invariably met by a good-looking young man and walked away with him. The presence of that young man was a source of passive satisfaction to Mr. Reeder, for no particular reason, unless it was that he had a tidy mind, and preferred a rose when it had a background of fern and grew uneasy at the sight of a saucerless cup.

It did not occur to him that he was an object of interest and curiosity to Miss Belman.

"That was Mr. Reeder—he has something to do with the police, I think," she said.

"Mr. J. G. Reeder?"

Roy Master looked back with interest at the middle-aged man scampering fearfully across the road, his unusual hat on the back of his head, his umbrella over his shoulder like a cavalryman's sword.

"Good Lord! I never dreamt he was like that."

"Who is he?" she asked, distracted from her own problem.

"Reeder? He's in the Public Prosecutor's Department, a sort of a detective—there was a case the other week where he gave evidence. He used to be with the Bank of England——"

Suddenly she stopped, and he looked at her in surprise.

"What's the matter?" he asked.

"I don't want you to go any farther, Roy," she said. "Mr. Telfer saw me with you yesterday, and he's quite unpleasant about it."

"Telfer?" said the young man indignantly. "That little worm! What did he say?"

"Nothing very much," she replied, but from her tone he gathered that the "nothing very much" had been a little disturbing.

"I am leaving Telfers'," she said unexpectedly. "It is a good job, and I shall never get another like it—I mean, so far as the pay is concerned."

Roy Master did not attempt to conceal his satisfaction.

"I'm jolly glad," he said vigorously. "I can't imagine how you've endured that boudoir atmosphere so long. What did he say?" he asked again, and, before she could answer: "Anyway, Telfers are shaky. There are all sorts of queer rumours about them in the city."

"But I thought it was a very rich corporation!" she said in astonishment. He shook his head.

"It was—but they have been doing lunatic things—what can you expect when a half-witted weakling like Sidney Telfer is at the head of affairs? They underwrote three concerns last year that no brokerage business would have touched with a barge-pole, and they had to take up the shares. One was a lost treasure company to raise a Spanish galleon that sank three hundred years ago! But what really did happen yesterday morning?"

"I will tell you to-night," she said, and made her hasty adieux.

Mr. Sidney Telfer had arrived when she went into a room which, in its luxurious appointments, its soft carpet and dainty etceteras, was not wholly undeserving of Roy Master's description.

The head of Telfers Consolidated seldom visited his main office on Threadneedle Street. The atmosphere of the place, he said, depressed him; it was all so horrid and sordid and rough. The founder of the firm, his grandfather, had died ten years before Sidney had been born, leaving the business to a son, a chronic invalid, who had died a few weeks after Sidney first saw the light. In the hands of trustees the business had flourished, despite the spasmodic interferences of his eccentric mother, whose peculiarities culminated in a will which relieved him of most of that restraint which is wisely laid upon a boy of sixteen.

The room, with its stained-glass windows and luxurious furnishings, fitted Mr. Telfer perfectly, for he was exquisitely arrayed. He was tall and so painfully thin that the abnormal smallness of his head was not at first apparent. As the girl came into the room he was sniffing delicately at a fine cambric handkerchief, and she thought that he was paler than she had ever seen him—and more repellent.

He followed her movements with a dull stare, and she had placed his letters on his table before he spoke.

"I say, Miss Belman, you won't mention a word about what I said to you last night?"

"Mr. Telfer," she answered quietly, "I am hardly likely to discuss such a matter."

"I'd marry you and all that, only . . . clause in my mother's will," he said disjointedly. "That could be got over—in time."

She stood by the table, her hands resting on the edge.

"I would not marry you, Mr. Telfer, even if there were no clause in your mother's will; the suggestion that I should run away with you to America——"

"South America," he corrected her gravely. "Not the United States; there was never any suggestion of the United States."

She could have smiled, for she was not as angry with this rather vacant young man as his startling proposition entitled her to be.

"The point is," he went on anxiously, "you'll keep it to yourself? I've been worried dreadfully all night. I told you to send me a note saying what you thought of my idea—well, don't!"

This time she did smile, but before she could answer him he went on, speaking rapidly in a high treble that sometimes rose to a falsetto squeak:

"You're a perfectly beautiful girl, and I'm crazy about you, but . . . there's a tragedy in my life . . . really. Perfectly ghastly tragedy. An' everything's at sixes an' sevens. If I'd had any sense I'd have brought in a feller to look after things. I'm beginning to see that now."

For the second time in twenty-four hours this young man, who had almost been tongue-tied and had never deigned to notice her, had poured forth a torrent of confidences, and in one had, with frantic insistence, set forth a plan which had amazed and shocked her. Abruptly he finished, wiped his weak eyes, and in his normal voice:

"Get Billingham on the 'phone; I want him."

She wondered, as her busy fingers flew over the keys of her typewriter, to what extent his agitation and wild eloquence was due to the rumoured "shakiness" of Telfers Consolidated.

Mr. Billingham came, a sober little man, bald and taciturn, and went in his secretive way into his employer's room. There was no hint in his appearance or his manner that he contemplated a great crime. He was stout to a point of podginess; apart from his habitual frown, his round face, unlined by the years, was marked by an expression of benevolence.

Yet Mr. Stephen Billingham, managing director of the Telfer Consolidated Trust, went into the office of the London and Central Bank late that afternoon and, presenting a bearer check for one hundred and fifty thousand pounds, which was duly honoured, was driven to the Crédit

Lilloise. He had telephoned particulars of his errand, and there were waiting for him seventeen packets, each containing a million francs, and a smaller packet of a hundred and forty-six *mille* notes. The franc stood at 74.55 and he received the eighteen packages in exchange for a check on the Crédit Lilloise for £80,000 and the 150 thousand-pound notes which he had drawn on the London and Central.

Of Billingham's movements thenceforth little was known. He was seen by an acquaintance driving through Cheapside in a taxicab which was traced as far as Charing Cross—and there he disappeared. Neither the airways nor the waterways had known him, the police theory being that he had left by an evening train that had carried an excursion party via Havre to Paris.

"This is the biggest steal we have had in years," said the Assistant Director of Public Prosecutions. "If you can slip in sideways on the inquiry, Mr. Reeder, I should be glad. Don't step on the toes of the city police—they are quite amiable people where murder is concerned, but a little touchy where money is in question. Go along and see Sidney Telfer."

Fortunately, the prostrated Sidney was discoverable outside the city area. Mr. Reeder went into the outer office and saw a familiar face.

"Pardon me, I think I know you, young lady," he said, and she smiled as she opened the little wooden gate to admit him.

"You are Mr. Reeder—we live in the same road," she said, and then quickly: "Have you come about Mr. Billingham?"

"Yes." His voice was hushed, as though he were speaking of a dead friend. "I wanted to see Mr. Telfer, but perhaps you could give me a little information."

The only news she had was that Sidney Telfer had been in the office since seven o'clock and was at the moment in such a state of collapse that she had sent for the doctor.

"I doubt if he is in a condition to see you," she said.

"I will take all responsibility," said Mr. Reeder soothingly. "Is Mr. Telfer—er—a friend of yours, Miss——?"

"Belman is my name." He had seen the quick flush that came to her cheek: it could mean one of two things. "No, I am an employee, that is all."

Her tone told him all he wanted to know. Mr. J. G. Reeder was something of an authority on office friendships.

"Bothered you a little, has he?" he murmured, and she shot a suspicious look at him. What did he know, and what bearing had Mr. Telfer's mad proposal on the present disaster? She was entirely in the dark as to the true state of affairs; it was, she felt, a moment for frankness.

"Wanted you to run away! Dear me!" Mr. Reeder was shocked. "He is married?"

"Oh, no—he's not married," said the girl shortly. "Poor man, I'm sorry for him now. I'm afraid that the loss is a very heavy one—who would suspect Mr. Billingham?"

"Ah! who indeed!" sighed the lugubrious Reeder, and took off his glasses to wipe them; almost she suspected tears. "I think I will go in now—that is the door?"

Sidney jerked up his face and glared at the intruder. He had been sitting with his head on his arms for the greater part of an hour.

"I say . . . what do you want?" he asked feebly. "I say . . . I can't see anybody . . . Public Prosecutor's Department?" He almost screamed the words. "What's the use of prosecuting him if you don't get the money back?"

Mr. Reeder let him work down before he began to ply his very judicious questions.

"I don't know much about it," said the despondent young man. "I'm only a sort of figurehead. Billingham brought the checks for me to sign and I signed 'em. I never gave him instructions; he got his orders. I don't know very much about it. He told me, actually told me, that the business was in a bad way—half a million or something was wanted by next week. . . . Oh, my God! And then he took the whole of our cash."

Sidney Telfer sobbed his woe into his sleeve like a child. Mr. Reeder waited before he asked a question in his gentlest manner.

"No, I wasn't here: I went down to Brighton for the week-end. And the police dug me out of bed at four in the morning. We're bankrupt. I'll have to sell my car and resign from my club—one has to resign when one is bankrupt."

There was little more to learn from the broken man, and Mr. Reeder returned to his chief with a report that added nothing to the sum of knowledge. In a week the theft of Mr. Billingham passed from scare lines to paragraphs in most of the papers—Billingham had made a perfect getaway.

In the bright lexicon of Mr. J. G. Reeder there was no such word as holiday. Even the Public Prosecutor's office has its slack time, when juniors and sub-officials and even the Director himself can go away on vacation, leaving the office open and a subordinate in charge. But to Mr. J. G. Reeder the very idea of wasting time was repugnant, and it was his practice to brighten the dull patches of occupation by finding a seat in a magistrate's court and listening, absorbed, to cases which bored even the court reporter.

John Smith, charged with being drunk and using insulting language to Police Officer Thomas Brown; Mary Jane Haggitt, charged with obstructing the police in the execution of their duty; Henry Robinson, arraigned for being a suspected person, having in his possession housebreaking tools, to wit, one cold chisel and a screwdriver; Arthur Moses, charged with driving a motor car to the common danger—all these were fascinating figures of romance and legend to the lean man who sat between the press and railed dock, his square-crowned hat by his side, his umbrella gripped between his knees, and on his melancholy face an expression of startled wonder.

On one raw and foggy morning, Mr. Reeder, self-released from his duties, chose the Marylebone Police Court for his recreation. Two drunks, a shop theft, and an embezzlement had claimed his rapt attention, when Mrs. Jackson was escorted to the dock and a rubicund policeman stepped to the witness stand, and, swearing by his Deity that he would tell the truth and nothing but the truth, related his peculiar story.

"P.C. Perryman No. 9717 L. Division," he introduced himself conventionally. "I was on duty in the Edgware Road early this morning at 2.30 a.m. when I saw the prisoner carrying a large suit-case. On seeing me she turned round and walked rapidly in the opposite direction. Her movements being suspicious, I followed and, overtaking her, asked her whose property she was carrying. She told me it was her own and that she was going to catch a train. She said that the case contained her clothes. As the case was a valuable one of crocodile leather I asked her to show me the inside. She refused. She also refused to give me her name and I asked her to accompany me to the station."

There followed a detective sergeant.

"I saw the prisoner at the station and in her presence opened the case. It contained a considerable quantity of small stone chips——"

"Stone chips?" interrupted the incredulous magistrate. "You mean small pieces of stone—what kind of stone?"

"Marble, your worship. She said that she wanted to make a little path in her garden and that she had taken them from the yard of a monument mason in the Euston Road. She made a frank statement to the effect that she had broken open a gate into the yard and filled the suit-case without the mason's knowledge."

The magistrate leant back in his chair and scrutinised the charge sheet with a frown.

"There is no address against her name," he said.

"She gave an address, but it was false, your worship—she refuses to offer any further information."

Mr. J. G. Reeder had screwed round in his seat and was staring open-mouthed at the prisoner. She was tall, broad-shouldered, and stoutly built. The hand that rested on the rail of the dock was twice the size of any woman's hand he had ever seen. The face was modelled largely, but though there was something in her appearance which was almost repellent, she was handsome in her large way. Deep-set brown eyes, a nose that was large and masterful, a well-shaped mouth and two chins—these in profile were not attractive to one who had his views on beauty in women, but Mr. J. G. Reeder, being a fair man, admitted that she was a fine-looking woman. When she spoke it was in a voice as deep as a man's, sonorous and powerful.

"I admit it was a fool thing to do. But the idea occurred to me just as I was going to bed and I acted on the impulse of the moment. I could well afford to buy the stone—I had over fifty pounds in my pocketbook when I was arrested."

"Is that true?" and, when the officer answered, the magistrate turned his suspicious eyes to the woman. "You are giving us a lot of trouble because you will not tell your name and address. I can understand that you do not wish your friends to know of your stupid theft, but unless you give me the information, I shall be compelled to remand you in custody for a week."

She was well, if plainly, dressed. On one large finger flashed a diamond which Mr. Reeder mentally priced in the region of two hundred pounds. "Mrs. Jackson" was shaking her head as he looked.

"I can't give you my address," she said, and the magistrate nodded curtly.

"Remanded for inquiry," he said, and added, as she walked out of the dock: "I should like a report from the prison doctor on the state of her mind."

Mr. J. G. Reeder rose quickly from his chair and followed the woman and the officer in charge of the case through the little door that leads to the cells.

"Mrs. Jackson" had disappeared by the time he reached the corridor, but the detective-sergeant was stooping over the large and handsome suitcase that he had shown in court and was now laying on a form.

Most of the outdoor men of the C.I.D. knew Mr. J. G. Reeder, and Sergeant Mills grinned a cheerful welcome.

"What do you think of that one, Mr. Reeder? It is certainly a new line on me! Never heard of a tombstone artist being burgled before."

He opened the top of the case, and Mr. Reeder ran his fingers through the marble chips.

"The case and the loot weighs over a hundred pounds," said the officer. "She must have the strength of a navvy to carry it. The poor officer who carried it to the station was hot and melting when he arrived."

Mr. J. G. was inspecting the case. It was a handsome article, the hinges and locks being of oxidised silver. No maker's name was visible on the inside, or owner's initials on its glossy lid. The lining had once been of silk, but now hung in shreds and was white with marble dust.

"Yes," said Mr. Reeder absently, "very interesting—most interesting. Is it permissible to ask whether, when she was searched, any—er—document—?" The sergeant shook his head. "Or unusual possession?"

"Only these."

By the side of the case was a pair of large gloves. These also were soiled, and their surfaces cut in a hundred places.

"These have been used frequently for the same purpose," murmured Mr. J. G. "She evidently makes—er—a collection of marble shavings. Nothing in her pocketbook?"

"Only the bank-notes: they have the stamp of the Central Bank on their backs. We should be able to trace 'em easily."

Mr. Reeder returned to his office and, locking the door, produced a worn pack of cards from a drawer and played patience—which was his method of thinking intensively. Late in the afternoon his telephone bell rang, and he recognised the voice of Sergeant Mills.

"Can I come along and see you? Yes, it is about the bank-notes."

Ten minutes later the sergeant presented himself.

"The notes were issued three months ago to Mr. Telfer," said the officer without preliminary, "and they were given by him to his housekeeper, Mrs. Welford."

"Oh, indeed?" said Mr. Reeder softly, and added, after reflection: "Dear me!"

He pulled hard at his lip.

"And is 'Mrs. Jackson' that lady?" he asked.

"Yes. Telfer—poor little devil—nearly went mad when I told him she was under remand—dashed up to Holloway in a taxi to identify her. The magistrate has granted bail, and she'll be bound over to-morrow. Telfer was bleating like a child—said she was mad. Gosh! that fellow is scared of her—when I took him into the waiting-room at Holloway Prison she gave him one look and he wilted. By the way, we have had a hint about Billingham that may interest you. Do you know that he and Telfer's secretary were very good friends?"

"Really?" Mr. Reeder was indeed interested. "Very good friends? Well, well!"

"The Yard has put Miss Belman under general observation: there may be nothing to it, but in cases like Billingham's it is very often a matter of *cherchez la femme!*"

Mr. Reeder had given his lip a rest and was now gently massaging his nose.

"Dear me!" he said. "That is a French expression, is it not?"

He was not in court when the marble stealer was sternly admonished by the magistrate and discharged. All that interested Mr. J. G. Reeder was to learn that the woman had paid the mason and had carried away her marble chips in triumph to the pretty little detached residence in the Outer Circle of Regent's Park. He had spent the morning at Somerset House, examining copies of wills and the like; his afternoon he gave up to the tracing of Mrs. Rebecca Alamby Mary Welford.

She was the relict of Professor John Welford of the University of Edinburgh, and had been left a widow after two years of marriage. She had then entered the service of Mrs. Telfer, the mother of Sidney, and had sole charge of the boy from his fourth year. When Mrs. Telfer died she had made the woman sole guardian of her youthful charge. So that Rebecca Welford had been by turns nurse and guardian, and was now in control of the young man's establishment.

The house occupied Mr. Reeder's attention to a considerable degree. It was a red-brick modern dwelling consisting of two floors and having a frontage on the Circle and a side road. Behind and beside the house was a large garden which, at this season of the year, was bare of flowers. They were probably in snug quarters for the winter, for there was a long greenhouse behind the garden.

He was leaning over the wooden palings, eyeing the grounds through the screen of box hedge that overlapped the fence with a melancholy stare, when he saw a door open and the big woman come out. She was barearmed and wore an apron. In one hand she carried a dust box, which she emptied into a concealed ashbin, in the other was a long broom.

Mr. Reeder moved swiftly out of sight. Presently the door slammed and he peeped again. There was no evidence of a marble path. All the walks were of rolled gravel.

He went to a neighbouring telephone booth, and called his office.

"I may be away all day," he said.

There was no sign of Mr. Sidney Telfer, though the detective knew that he was in the house.

Telfer's Trust was in the hands of the liquidators, and the first meeting of creditors had been called. Sidney had, by all accounts, been confined to his bed, and from that safe refuge had written a note to his secretary asking that "all papers relating to my private affairs" should be burnt. He had scrawled a postscript: "Can I possibly see you on business before I go?" The word "go" had been scratched out and "retire" substituted. Mr. Reeder had seen that letter—indeed, all correspondence between Sidney and the office came to him by arrangement with the liquidators. And that was partly why Mr. J. G. Reeder was so interested in 904, The Circle.

It was dusk when a big car drew up at the gate of the house. Before the driver could descend from his seat, the door of 904 opened, and Sidney Telfer almost ran out. He carried a suit-case in each hand, and Mr. Reeder recognised that nearest him as the grip in which the housekeeper had carried the stolen marble.

Reaching over, the chauffeur opened the door of the machine and, flinging in the bags, Sidney followed hastily. The door closed, and the car went out of sight round the curve of The Circle.

Mr. Reeder crossed the road and took up a position very near the front gate, waiting.

Dusk came and the veil of a Regent's Park fog. The house was in darkness, no flash of light except a faint glimmer that burnt in the hall, no sound. The woman was still there—Mrs. Sidney Telfer, nurse, companion, guardian and wife. Mrs. Sidney Telfer, the hidden director of Telfers Consolidated, a masterful woman who, not content with marrying a weakling twenty years her junior, had applied her masterful but ill-equipped mind to the domination of a business she did not understand, and which she was destined to plunge into ruin. Mr. Reeder had made good use of his time at the Records Office: a copy of the marriage certificate was almost as easy to secure as a copy of the will.

He glanced round anxiously. The fog was clearing, which was exactly what he did not wish it to do, for he had certain acts to perform which required as thick a cloaking as possible.

And then a surprising thing happened. A cab came slowly along the road and stopped at the gate.

"I think this is the place, miss," said the cabman, and a girl stepped down to the pavement.

It was Miss Margaret Belman.

Reeder waited until she had paid the fare and the cab had gone, and then, as she walked toward the gate, he stepped from the shadow.

"Oh!—Mr. Reeder, how you frightened me!" she gasped. "I am going to see Mr. Telfer—he is dangerously ill—no, it was his housekeeper who wrote asking me to come at seven."

"Did she now! Well, I will ring the bell for you."

She told him that that was unnecessary—she had the key which had come with the note.

"She is alone in the house with Mr. Telfer, who refuses to allow a trained nurse near him," said Margaret, "and——"

"Will you be good enough to lower your voice, young lady?" urged Mr. Reeder in an impressive whisper. "Forgive the impertinence, but if our friend is ill——"

She was at first startled by his urgency.

"He couldn't hear me," she said, but spoke in a lower tone.

"He may—sick people are very sensitive to the human voice. Tell me, how did this letter come?"

"From Mr. Telfer? By district messenger an hour ago."

Nobody had been to the house or left it—except Sidney. And Sidney, in his blind fear, would carry out any instructions which his wife gave to him.

"And did it contain a passage like this?" Mr. Reeder considered a moment. " 'Bring this letter with you'?"

"No," said the girl in surprise, "but Mrs. Welford telephoned just before the letter arrived and told me to wait for it. And she asked me to bring the letter with me because she didn't wish Mr. Telfer's private correspondence to be left lying around. But why do you ask me this, Mr. Reeder—is anything wrong?"

He did not answer immediately. Pushing open the gate, he walked noiselessly along the grass plot that ran parallel with the path.

"Open the door, I will come in with you," he whispered and, when she hesitated: "Do as I tell you, please."

The hand that put the key into the lock trembled, but at last the key turned and the door swung open. A small night-light burnt on the table of the wide panelled hall. On the left, near the foot of the stairs, only the lower steps of which were visible, Reeder saw a narrow door which stood open, and, taking a step forward, saw that it was a tiny telephone-room.

And then a voice spoke from the upper landing, a deep, booming voice that he knew.

"Is that Miss Belman?"

Margaret, her heart beating faster, went to the foot of the stairs and looked up.

"Yes, Mrs. Welford."

"You brought the letter with you?"

"Yes."

Mr. Reeder crept along the wall until he could have touched the girl.

"Good," said the deep voice. "Will you call the doctor—Circle 743—and tell him that Mr. Telfer has had a relapse—you will find the booth in the hall: shut the door behind you, the bell worries him."

Margaret looked at the detective and he nodded.

The woman upstairs wished to gain time for something—what?

The girl passed him: he heard the thud of the padded door close, and there was a click that made him spin round. The first thing he noticed was that there was no handle to the door, the second that the keyhole was covered by a steel disc, which he discovered later was felt-lined. He heard the girl speaking faintly, and put his ear to the keyhole.

"The instrument is disconnected—I can't open the door."

Without a second's hesitation, he flew up the stairs, umbrella in hand, and as he reached the landing he heard a door close with a crash. Instantly he located the sound. It came from a room on the left immediately over the hall. The door was locked.

"Open this door," he commanded, and there came to him the sound of a deep laugh.

Mr. Reeder tugged at the stout handle of his umbrella. There was a flicker of steel as he dropped the lower end, and in his hand appeared six inches of knife blade.

The first stab at the panel sliced through the thin wood as though it were paper. In a second there was a jagged gap through which the black muzzle of an automatic was thrust.

"Put down that jug or I will blow your features into comparative chaos!" said Mr. Reeder pedantically.

The room was brightly lit, and he could see plainly. Mrs. Welford stood by the side of a big square funnel, the narrow end of which ran into the floor. In her hand was a huge enamelled iron jug, and ranged about her were six others. In one corner of the room was a wide circular tank, and beyond, at half its height, depended a large copper pipe.

The woman's face turned to him was blank, expressionless.

"He wanted to run away with her," she said simply, "and after all I have done for him!"

"Open the door."

Mrs. Welford set down the jug and ran her huge hand across her forehead.

"Sidney is my own darling," she said. "I've nursed him, and taught him, and there was a million—all in gold—in the ship. But they robbed him."

She was talking of one of the ill-fated enterprises of Telfers Consolidated Trust—that sunken treasure ship to recover which the money of the company had been poured out like water. And she was mad. He had guessed the weakness of this domineering woman from the first.

"Open the door; we will talk it over. I'm perfectly sure that the treasure ship scheme was a sound one."

"Are you?" she asked eagerly, and the next minute the door was open and Mr. J. G. Reeder was in that room of death.

"First of all, let me have the key of the telephone-room—you are quite wrong about that young lady: she is my wife."

The woman stared at him blankly.

"Your wife?" A slow smile transfigured the face. "Why—I was silly.

Here is the key.''

He persuaded her to come downstairs with him, and when the frightened girl was released, he whispered a few words to her, and she flew out of the house.

"Shall we go into the drawing-room?'' he asked, and Mrs. Welford led the way.

"And now will you tell me how you knew—about the jugs?'' he asked gently.

She was sitting on the edge of a sofa, her hands clasped on her knees, her deep-set eyes staring at the carpet.

"John—that was my first husband—told me. He was a professor of chemistry and natural science, and also about the electric furnace. It is so easy to make if you have power—we use nothing but electricity in this house for heating and everything. And then I saw my poor darling being ruined through me, and I found how much money there was in the bank, and I told Billingham to draw it and bring it to me without Sidney knowing. He came here in the evening. I sent Sidney away—to Brighton, I think. I did everything—put the new lock on the telephone box and fixed the shaft from the roof to the little room—it was easy to disperse everything with all the doors open and an electric fan working on the floor——''

She was telling him about the improvised furnace in the green-house when the police arrived with the divisional surgeon, and she went away with them, weeping because there would be nobody to press Sidney's ties or put out his shirts.

Mr. Reeder took the inspector up to the little room and showed him its contents.

"This funnel leads to the telephone box——'' he began.

"But the jugs are empty,'' interrupted the officer.

Mr. J. G. Reeder struck a match and, waiting until it burnt freely, lowered it into the jug. Half an inch lower than the rim the light went out.

"Carbon monoxide,'' he said, "which is made by steeping marble chips in hydrochloric acid—you will find the mixture in the tank. The gas is colourless and odourless—and heavy. You can pour it out of a jug like water. She could have bought the marble, but was afraid of arousing suspicion. Billingham was killed that way. She got him to go to the telephone box, probably closed the door on him herself, and then killed him painlessly.''

"What did she do with the body?'' asked the horrified officer.

"Come out into the hot-house,'' said Mr. Reeder, "and pray do not expect to see horrors: an electric furnace will dissolve a diamond to its original elements.''

*　　*　　*　　*　　*

The Stealer of Marble

Mr. Reeder went home that night in a state of mental perturbation, and for an hour paced the floor of his large study in Brockley Road.

Over and over in his mind he turned one vital problem: did he owe an apology to Margaret Belman for saying that she was his wife?

V

Sheer Melodrama

It was Mr. Reeder who planned the raid on Tommy Fenalow's snide shop and worked out all the details except the composition of the raiding force. Tommy had a depot at Golders Green whither trusted agents came, purchasing £1 Treasury notes for £7 10s. per hundred, or £70 a thousand. Only experts could tell the difference between Tommy's currency and that authorised by and printed for H.M. Treasury. They were the right shades of brown and green, the numbers were of issued series, the paper was exact. They were printed in Germany at £3 a thousand, and Tommy made thousands per cent. profit.

Mr. Reeder discovered all about Tommy's depot in his spare time, and reported the matter to his chief, the Director of Public Prosecutions. From Whitehall to Scotland Yard is two minutes' walk, and in just that time the information got across.

"Take Inspector Greyash with you and superintend the raid," were his instructions.

He left the inspector to make all the arrangements, and amongst those who learnt of the projected coup was a certain detective officer who made more money from questionable associations than he did from Government. This officer "blew" the raid to Tommy, and when Mr. Reeder and his bold men arrived at Golders Green, there was Tommy and three friends playing a quiet game of auction bridge, and the only Treasury notes discoverable were veritable old masters.

"It is a pity," sighed J. G. when they reached the street: "a great pity. Of course I hadn't the least idea that Detective-Constable Wilshore was in our party. He is—er—not quite loyal."

"Wilshore?" asked the officer, aghast. "Do you mean he 'blew' the raid to Tommy?"

Mr. Reeder scratched his nose and said gently that he thought so.

"He has quite a big income from various sources—by the way, he banks with the Midland and Derbyshire, and his account is in his wife's maiden name. I tell you this in case—er—it may be useful."

It was useful enough to secure the summary ejection of the unfaithful

Wilshore from the force, but it was not sufficiently useful to catch Tommy, whose parting words were: "You're clever, Reeder; but you've got to be *lucky* to catch me!"

Tommy was in the habit of repeating this scrap of conversation to such as were interested. It was an encounter of which he was justifiably proud, for few dealers in "slush" and "snide" have ever come up against Mr. J. G. and got away with it.

"It's worth a thousand pounds to me—ten thousand! I'd pay that money to make J. G. look sick, anyway, the old dog! I guess the Yard will think twice before it tries to shop me again, and that's the real kick in the raid. J. G.'s name is Jonah at headquarters, and if I can do anything to help, it will be mud!"

To a certain Ras Lal Punjabi, an honoured (and paying) guest, Mr. Fenalow told this story, with curious results.

A good wine tastes best in its own country, and a man may drink sherry by the cask in Jerez de la Frontera and take no ill, whereas if he attempted so much as a bottle in Fleet Street, he would suffer cruelly. So also does the cigarette of Egypt preserve its finest bouquet for such as smoke it in the lounge of a Cairo hotel.

Crime is yet another quantity which does not bear transplanting. The American safe-blower may flourish in France just so long as he acquires by diligent study, and confines himself to, the Continental method. It is possible for the European thief to gain a fair livelihood in oriental countries, but there is no more tragic sight in the world than the Eastern mind endeavouring to adapt itself to the complexities of European roguery.

Ras Lal Punjabi enjoyed a reputation in Indian police circles as the cleverest native criminal India had ever produced. Beyond a short term in Poona Jail, Ras Lal had never seen the interior of a prison, and such was his fame in native circles that, during this short period of incarceration, prayers for his deliverance were offered at certain temples, and it was agreed that he would never have been convicted at all but for some pretty hard swearing on the part of the police commissioner *sahib*—and anyway, all *sahibs* hang together, and it was a European judge who sent him down.

He was a general practitioner of crime, with a leaning toward specialisation in jewel thefts. A man of excellent and even gentlemanly appearance, with black and shiny hair parted at the side and curling up over one brow in an inky wave, he spoke English, Hindustani, and Tamil very well indeed, had a sketchy knowledge of the law (on his visiting cards was the inscription "Failed LL.B.") and a very full acquaintance with the science of precious stones.

During Mr. Ras Lal Punjabi's brief rest in Poona, the police commissioner *sahib*, whose unromantic name was Smith, married a not very good-looking girl with a lot of money. Smith Sahib knew that beauty was only skin deep and that she had a kind heart, which is notoriously preferable to the garniture of coronets. It was honestly a love match. Her father owned jute mills in Calcutta, and on festive occasions, such as the Governor-General's ball, she carried several lakhs of rupees on her person; but even rich people are loved for themselves alone.

Ras Lal owed his imprisonment to an unsuccessful attempt he had made upon two strings of pearls the property of the lady in question, and when he learnt, on his return to freedom, that Smith Sahib had married the resplendent girl and had gone to England, he very naturally attributed the hatred and bitterness of Smith Sahib to purely personal causes, and swore vengeance.

Now in India the business of every man is the business of his servants. The preliminary inquiries, over which an English or American jewel thief would spend a small fortune, can be made at the cost of a few annas. When Ras Lal came to England he found that he had overlooked this very important fact.

Smith, *Sahib* and *Memsahib*, were out of town; they were, in fact, on the high seas en route for New York when Ras Lal was arrested on the conventional charge of "being a suspected person." Ras had shadowed the Smiths' butler, and, having induced him to drink, had offered him immense sums to reveal the place, receptacle, drawer, safe, box, or casket where "Mrs. Commissioner Smith's" jewels were kept. His excuse for asking, namely, that he had had a wager with his brother that the jewels were kept under the *Memsahib's* bed, showed a lamentable lack of inventive power. The butler, an honest man, though a drinker of beer, informed the police. Ras Lal and his friend and assistant Ram were arrested, brought before a magistrate, and would have been discharged but for the fact that Mr. J. G. Reeder saw the record of the case and was able to supply from his own files very important particulars of the dark man's past. Therefore Mr. Ras Lal was sent down to hard labour for six months, but, what was more maddening, the story of his ignominious failure was, he guessed, broadcast throughout India.

This was the thought which distracted him in his lonely cell at Wormwood Scrubbs. What would India think of him?—he would be the scorn of the bazars, "the mocking point of third-rate mediocrities," to use his own expression. And automatically he switched his hate from Smith Sahib to one Mr. J. G. Reeder. And his hate was very real, more real because of the insignificance and unimportance of this Reeder Sahib, whom he likened to an ancient cow, a sneaking weasel, and other things less translatable. And in the six months of his durance he planned desperate and earnest acts of reprisal.

Released from prison, he decided that the moment was not ripe for a return to India. He wished to make a close study of Mr. J. G. Reeder and his habits, and, being a man with plenty of money, he could afford the time, and, as it happened, could mix business with pleasure.

Mr. Tommy Fenalow found means of getting in touch with the gentleman from the Orient whilst he was in Wormwood Scrubbs, and the handsome limousine that met Ras Lal at the gates of the Scrubbs when he came out of jail was both hired and occupied by Tommy, a keen business man, who had been offered by his German printer a new line of one-hundred-rupee notes that might easily develop into a most profitable side-line.

"You come along and lodge at my expense, boy," said the sympathetic Tommy, who was very short, very stout, and had eyes that bulged like a pug dog's. "You've been badly treated by old Reeder, and I'm going to tell you a way of getting back on him, with no risk and a ninety per cent. profit. Listen, a friend of mine . . ."

It was never Tommy who had snide for sale: invariably the hawker of forged notes was a mysterious "friend."

So Ras was lodged in a service flat which formed part of a block owned by Mr. Fenalow, who was a very rich man indeed. Some weeks after this, Tommy crossed St. James's Street to intercept his old enemy.

"Good-morning, Mr. Reeder."

Mr. J. G. Reeder stopped and turned back.

"Good-morning, Mr. Fenalow," he said, with that benevolent solicitude which goes so well with a frock-coat and square-toed shoes. "I am glad to see that you are out again, and I do trust that you will now find a more—er—legitimate outlet for your undoubted talents."

Tommy went angrily red.

"I haven't been in 'stir' and you know it, Reeder! It wasn't for want of trying on your part. But you've got to be something more than clever to catch me—you've got to be lucky! Not that there's anything to catch me over—I've never done a crooked thing in my life, as you well know."

He was so annoyed that the lighter exchanges of humour he had planned slipped from his memory.

He had an appointment with Ras Lal, and the interview was entirely satisfactory. Mr. Ras Lal made his way that night to an uncomfortably situated rendezvous and there met his new friend.

"This is the last place in the world old man Reeder would dream of searching," said Tommy enthusiastically, "and if he did he would find nothing. Before he could get into the building, the stuff would be put out of sight.''

It is a habitation of extreme convenience,'' said Ras Lal.

"It is yours, boy,'' replied Tommy magnificently. "I only keep this place to get-in and put-out. The stuff's not here for an hour and the rest of the time the store's empty. As I say, old man Reeder has gotta be something more than clever—he's gotta be lucky!''

At parting he handed his client a key, and with that necessary instrument tendered a few words of advice and warning.

"Never come here till late. The police patrol passes the end of the road at ten, one o'clock, and four. When are you leaving for India?''

"On the twenty-third,'' said Ras, "by which time I shall have uttered a few reprisals on that cad Reeder.''

"I shouldn't like to be in his shoes,'' said Tommy, who could afford to be sycophantic, for he had in his pocket two hundred pounds' worth of real money which Ras had paid in advance for a vaster quantity of money which was not so real.

It was a few days after this that Ras Lal went to the Orpheum Theatre, and it was no coincidence that he went there on the same night that Mr. Reeder escorted a pretty lady to the same place of amusement.

When Mr. J. G. Reeder went to the theatre (and his going at all was contingent upon his receiving a complimentary ticket) he invariably chose a melodrama, and preferably a Drury Lane melodrama, where to the thrill of the actors' speeches was added the amazing action of wrecked railway trains, hair-raising shipwrecks, and terrific horse-races in which the favourite won by a nose. Such things may seem wildly improbable to blasé dramatic critics—especially favourites winning—but Mr. Reeder saw actuality in all such presentations.

Once he was inveigled into sitting through a roaring farce, and was the only man in the house who did not laugh. He was, indeed, such a depressing influence that the leading lady sent a passionate request to the manager that "the miserable-looking old man in the middle of the front row'' should have his money returned and be requested to leave the theatre. Which, as Mr. Reeder had come in on a free ticket, placed the manager in a very awkward predicament.

Invariably he went unaccompanied, for he had no friends, and fifty-two years had come and gone without bringing to his life romance or the melting tenderness begot of dreams. In some manner Mr. Reeder had become acquainted with a girl who was like no other girl with whom he had been brought into contact. Her name was Belman, Margaret Belman, and he had saved her life, though this fact did not occur to him as frequently as the recollection that he had imperilled that life before he had saved it. And he had a haunting sense of guilt for quite another reason.

He was thinking of her one day—he spent his life thinking about people, though the majority of these were less respectable than Miss Margaret Belman. He supposed that she would marry the very good-looking young man who met her street car at the corner of the Embankment every morning and returned with her to the Lewisham High Road every night. It would be a very nice wedding, with hired motor-cars, and the vicar himself performing the ceremony, and a wedding breakfast provided by the local caterer, following which bride and bridegroom would be photographed on the lawn surrounded by their jovial but unprepossessing relatives. And after this, one specially hired car would take them to Eastbourne for an expensive honeymoon. And after that all the humdrum and scrapings of life, rising through villadom to a little car of their own and Saturday afternoon tennis parties.

Mr. Reeder sighed deeply. How much more satisfactory was the stage drama, where all the trouble begins in the first act and is satisfactorily settled in the last. He fingered absently the two slips of green paper that had come to him that morning. Row A, seats 17 and 18. They had been sent by a manager who was under some obligation to him. The theatre was the Orpheum home of transpontine drama, and the play was "The Fires of Vengeance." It looked like being a pleasant evening.

He took an envelope from the rack, addressed it to the box office, and had begun to write the accompanying letter returning the surplus voucher, when an idea occurred to him. He owed Miss Margaret Belman something, and the debt was on his conscience. He had once, for reasons of expediency, described her as his wife. This preposterous claim had been made to appease a mad woman, it is true, but it had been made. She was now holding a good position—a secretaryship at one of the political headquarters, for which post she had to thank Mr. J. G. Reeder, if she only knew it.

He took up the 'phone and called her number, and, after the normal delay, heard her voice.

"Er—Miss Belman," Mr. Reeder coughed, "I have—er two tickets for a theatre to-night. I wonder if you would care to go?"

Her astonishment was almost audible.

"That is very nice of you, Mr. Reeder. I should love to come with you."

Mr. J. G. Reeder turned pale.

"What I mean is, I have *two* tickets—I thought perhaps that your—er—your—er—that somebody else would like to go—what I mean was——"

He heard a gentle laugh at the other end of the 'phone.

"What you mean is that you don't wish to take me," she said, and for a man of his experience he blundered badly.

"I should esteem it an honour to take you," he said, in terror that he should offend her, "but the truth is, I thought——"

"I will meet you at the theatre—which is it? Orpheum—how lovely! At eight o'clock."

Mr. Reeder put down the instrument, feeling limp and moist. It is the truth that he had never taken a lady to any kind of social function in his life, and as there grew upon him the tremendous character of this adventure he was overwhelmed and breathless. A murderer waking from dreams of revelry to find himself in the condemned cell suffered no more poignant emotions than Mr. Reeder, torn from the smooth if treacherous currents of life and drawing nearer and nearer to the horrid vortex of unusualness.

"Bless me," said Mr. Reeder, employing a strictly private expression which was reserved for his own crises.

He employed in his private office a young woman who combined a meticulous exactness in the filing of documents with a complete absence of those attractions which turn men into gods and in other days set the armies of Perseus moving toward the walls of Troy. She was invariably addressed by Mr. Reeder as "Miss." He believed her name to be "Oliver." She was in truth a married lady with two children, but her nuptials had been celebrated without his knowledge.

To the top floor of a building in Regent Street Mr. Reeder repaired for instruction and guidance.

"It is not—er—a practice of mine to—er—accompany ladies to the theatre, and I am rather at a loss to know what is expected of me, the more so since the young lady is—er—a stranger to me."

His frosty-visaged assistant sneered secretly. At Mr. Reeder's time of life, when such natural affections as were not atrophied should in decency be fossilised!

He jotted down her suggestions.

"Chocolates indeed? Where can one procure——? Oh, yes, I remember seeing the attendants sell them. Thank you so much, Miss—er—"

And as he went out, closing the door carefully behind him, she sneered openly.

"They all go wrong at seventy," she said insultingly.

Margaret hardly knew what to expect when she came into the flamboyant foyer of the Orpheum. What was the evening equivalent to the square-topped derby and the tightly buttoned frock-coat of ancient design which he favoured in the hours of business? She would have passed the somewhat elegantly dressed gentleman in the correct piqué waistcoat and the perfectly tied butterfly bow, only he claimed her attention.

"Mr. Reeder!" she gasped.

It was indeed Mr. Reeder: with not so much as a shirt-stud wrong; with a suit of the latest mode, and shoes glossy and V-toed. For Mr. Reeder, like many other men, dressed according to his inclination in business hours, but accepted blindly the instructions of his tailor in the matter of fancy raiment. Mr. J. G. Reeder was never conscious of his clothing, good or bad—he was, however, very conscious of his strange responsibility.

He took her cloak (he had previously purchased programmes and a large box of chocolates, which he carried by its satin ribbon). There was a quarter of an hour to wait before the curtain went up, and Margaret felt it incumbent upon her to offer an explanation.

"You spoke about 'somebody' else; do you mean Roy—the man who sometimes meets me at Westminster?"

Mr. Reeder *had* meant that young man.

"He and I were good friends," she said, "no more than that—we aren't very good friends any more."

She did not say why. She might have explained in a sentence if she had said that Roy's mother held an exalted opinion of her only son's qualities, physical and mental, and that Roy thoroughly endorsed his mother's judgment, but she did not.

"Ah!" said Mr. Reeder unhappily.

Soon after this the orchestra drowned further conversation, for they were sitting in the first row near to the noisiest of the brass and not far removed from the shrillest of the woodwind. In odd moments, through the thrilling first act, she stole a glance at her companion. She expected to find this man mildly amused or slightly bored by the absurd contrast between the realities which he knew and the theatricalities which were presented on the stage. But whenever she looked, he was absorbed in the action of the play; she could almost feel him tremble when the hero was strapped to a log and thrown into the boiling mountain stream, and when the stage Jove was rescued on the fall of the curtain, she heard, with something like stupefaction, Mr. Reeder's quivering sigh of relief.

"But surely, Mr. Reeder, this bores you?" she protested, when the lights in the auditorium went up.

"This—you mean the play—bore me? Good gracious, no! I think it is very fine, remarkably fine."

"But it isn't life, surely? The story is so wildly improbable, and the incidents—oh, yes, I'm enjoying it all; please don't look so worried! Only I thought that you, who knew so much about criminology—is that the word?—would be rather amused."

Mr. Reeder was looking very anxiously at her.

"I'm afraid it is not the kind of play——"

"Oh, but it is—I love melodrama. But doesn't it strike you as being—far-fetched? For instance, that man being chained to a log, and the mother agreeing to her son's death?"

Mr. Reeder rubbed his nose thoughtfully.

"The Bermondsey gang chained Harry Salter to a plank, turned it over and let him drown, just opposite Billingsgate Market. I was at the execution of Tod Rowe, and he admitted it on the scaffold. And it was 'Lee' Pearson's mother who poisoned him at Teddington to get his insurance money so that she could marry again. I was at the trial and she took her sentence laughing—now what else was there in that act? Oh, yes, I remember: the proprietor of the saw-mill tried to get the young lady to marry him by threatening to send her father to prison. That has been done hundreds of times—only in a worse way. There is really nothing very extravagant about a melodrama except the prices of the seats, and I usually get my tickets free!"

She listened, at first dumbfounded and then with a gurgle of amusement.

"How queer—and yet—well, frankly, I have only met melodrama once in life, and even now I cannot believe it. What happens in the next act?"

Mr. Reeder consulted his programme.

"I rather believe that the young woman in the white dress is captured and removed to the harem of an Eastern potentate," he said precisely, and this time the girl laughed aloud.

"Have you a parallel for that?" she asked triumphantly, and Mr. Reeder was compelled to admit that he knew no exact parallel, but——

"It is rather a remarkable coincidence," he said, "a very remarkable coincidence!"

She looked at her programme, wondering if she had overlooked anything so very remarkable.

"There is at this moment, watching me from the front row of the dress circle—I beg you not to turn your head—one who, if he is not a potentate, is undoubtedly Eastern; there are in fact, two dark-complexioned gentlemen, but only one may be described as important."

"But why are they watching you?" she asked in surprise.

"Possibly," said Mr. Reeder solemnly, "because I look so remarkable in evening dress."

One of the dark-complexioned gentlemen turned to his companion at this moment.

"It is the woman he travels with every day; she lives in the same street, and is doubtless more to him than anybody in the world, Ram. See how she laughs in his face and how the old so-and-so looks at her! When men come to his great age they grow silly about women. This thing can be done to-night. I would sooner die than go back to Bombay without accomplishing my design upon this such-and-such and so-forth."

Ram, his chauffeur, confederate, and fellow jail-bird, who was cast in a less heroic mould, and had, moreover, no personal vendetta, suggested in haste that the matter should be thought over.

"I have cogitated every hypothesis to their logical conclusions," said Ras Lal in English.

"But, master," said his companion urgently, "would it not be wise to leave this country and make a fortune with the new money which the fat little man can sell to us?"

"Vengeance is mine," said Ras Lal in English.

He sat through the next act, which, as Mr. Reeder had truly said, depicted the luring of an innocent girl into the hateful clutches of a Turkish pasha and, watching the development of the plot, his own scheme underwent revision. He did not wait to see what happened in the third and fourth acts—there were certain preparations to be made.

"I still think that, whilst the story is awfully thrilling, it is awfully impossible," said Margaret, as they moved slowly through the crowded vestibule. "In real life—in civilised countries, I mean—masked men do not suddenly appear from nowhere with pistols and say 'Hands up!'—not really, do they, Mr. Reeder?" she coaxed.

Mr. Reeder murmured a reluctant agreement.

"But I have enjoyed it tremendously!" she said with enthusiasm, and looking down into the pink face Mr. Reeder felt a curious sensation which was not entirely pleasure and not wholly pain.

"I am very glad," he said.

Both the dress circle and the stalls disgorged into the foyer, and he was looking round for a face he had seen when he arrived. But neither Ras Lal nor his companion in misfortune was visible. Rain was falling dismally, and it was some time before he found a cab.

"Luxury upon luxury," smiled Margaret, when he took his place by her side. "You may smoke if you wish."

Mr. Reeder took a paper packet of cigarettes from his waistcoat pocket, selected a limp cylinder, and lit it.

"No plays are quite like life, my dear young lady," he said, as he carefully pushed the match through the space between the top of the window and the frame. "Melodramas appeal most to me because of their idealism."

She turned and stared at him.

"Idealism?" she repeated incredulously.

He nodded.

"Have you ever noticed that there is nothing sordid about a melodrama? I once saw a classical drama—'Œdipus'—and it made me feel sick. In melodrama even the villains are heroic, and the inevitable and unvarying moral is 'Truth crushed to earth will rise again'—isn't that idealism? And they are wholesome. There are no sex problems; unpleasant things are never shown in an attractive light—you come away uplifted."

"If you are young enough," she smiled.

"One should always be young enough to rejoice in the triumph of virtue," said Mr. Reeder soberly.

They crossed Westminster Bridge and bore left to the New Kent Road. Through the rain-blurred windows J. G. picked up the familiar landmarks and offered a running commentary upon them in the manner of a guide. Margaret had not realised before that history was made in South London.

"There used to be a gibbet here—this ugly-looking goods station was the London terminus of the first railways—Queen Alexandra drove from there when she came to be married—the thoroughfare on the right after we pass the Canal bridge is curiously named Bird-in-Bush Road——"

A big car had drawn level with the cab, and the driver was shouting something to the cabman. Even the suspicious Mr. Reeder suspected no more than an exchange of offensiveness, till the cab suddenly turned into the road he had been speaking about. The car had fallen behind, but now drew abreast.

"Probably the main road is up," said J. G., and at that moment the cab slowed and stopped.

He was reaching out for the handle when the door was pulled open violently, and in the uncertain light Mr. Reeder saw a broad-shouldered man standing in the road.

"Alight quickly!"

In the man's hand was a long black Colt, and his face was covered from chin to forehead by a mask.

"Quickly—and keep your hands erect!"

Mr. Reeder stepped out into the rain and reached to close the door.

"The female also—come, miss!"

"Here—what's the game—you told me the New Cross Road was blocked." It was the cabman talking.

"Here is a five—keep your mouth shut."

The masked man thrust a note at the driver.

"I don't want your money——"

"You require my bullet in your bosom perchance, my good fellow?" asked Ras Lal sardonically.

Margaret had followed her escort into the road by this time. The car had stopped just behind the cab. With the muzzle of the pistol stuck into his back, Mr. Reeder walked to the open door and entered. The girl followed, and the masked man jumped after them and closed the door. Instantly the interior was flooded with light.

"This is a considerable surprise to a clever and intelligent police detective?"

Their captor sat on the opposite seat, his pistol on his knees. Through the holes of the black mask a pair of brown eyes gleamed malevolently. But Mr. Reeder's interest was in the girl. The shock had struck the colour from her face, but he observed with thankfulness that her chief emotion was not fear. She was numb with amazement, and was stricken speechless.

The car had circled and was moving swiftly back the way they had come. He felt the rise of the Canal bridge, and then the machine turned abruptly to the right and began the descent of a steep hill. They were running toward Rotherhithe—he had an extraordinary knowledge of London's topography.

The journey was a short one. He felt the car wheels bump over an uneven roadway for a hundred yards, the body rocking uncomfortably, and then with a jar of brakes the machine stopped suddenly.

They were on a narrow muddy lane. On one side rose the arches of a railway aqueduct, on the other an open space bounded by a high fence. Evidently the driver had pulled up short of their destination, for they had to squelch and slide through the thick mud for another fifty yards before they came to a narrow gateway in the fence. Through this they struck a cinder-path leading to a square building, which Mr. Reeder guessed was a small factory of some kind. Their conductor flashed a lamp on the door, and in weather-worn letters the detective read:

"The Storn-Filton Leather Company."

"Now!" said the man, as he turned a switch. "Now, my false-swearing and corrupt police official, I have a slight bill to settle with you."

They were in a dusty lobby, enclosed on three sides by matchboard walls.

" 'Account' is the word you want, Ras Lal," murmured Mr. Reeder.

For a moment the man was taken aback, and then, snatching the mask from his face:

"I am Ras Lal! And you shall repent it! For you and your young missus this is indeed a cruel night of anxiety!"

Mr. Reeder did not smile at the quaint English. The gun in the man's hand spoke all languages without error, and could be as fatal in the hands of an unconscious humorist as if it were handled by the most savage of purists. And he was worried about the girl: she had not spoken a word since their capture. The colour had come back to her cheeks, and that was a good sign.

67

There was, too, a light in her eyes which Reeder could not associate with fear.

Ras Lal, taking down a long cord that hung on a nail in the wooden partition, hesitated.

"It is not necessary," he said, with an elaborate shrug of shoulder; "the room is sufficiently reconnoitred—you will be innocuous there."

Flinging open a door, he motioned them to pass through and mount the bare stairs which faced them. At the top was a landing and a large steel door set in the solid brickwork.

Pulling back the iron bolt, he pushed at the door, and it opened with a squeak. It was a large room, and had evidently been used for the storage of something inflammable, for the walls and floor were of rough-faced concrete and above a dusty desk an inscription was painted, "Danger. Don't smoke in this store." There were no windows except one some eighteen inches square, the top of which was near the ceiling. In one corner of the room was a heap of grimy paper files, and on the desk a dozen small wooden boxes, one of which had been opened, for the nail-bristling lid was canted up at an angle.

"Make yourself content for half an hour or probably forty minutes," said Ras Lal, standing in the doorway with his ostentatious revolver. "At that time I shall come for your female; to-morrow she will be on a ship with me, bound for—ah, who knows where?"

"Shut the door as you go out," said Mr. J. G. Reeder; "there is an unpleasant draught."

Mr. Tommy Fenalow came on foot at two o'clock in the morning and, passing down the muddy lane, his electric torch suddenly revealed car marks. Tommy stopped like a man shot. His knees trembled beneath him and his heart entered his throat at the narrowest end. For a while he was undecided whether it would be better to run or walk away. He had no intention of going forward. And then he heard a voice. It was Ras Lal's assistant, and he nearly swooned with joy. Stumbling forward, he came up to the shivering man.

"Did that fool boss of yours bring the car along here?" he asked in a whisper.

"Yas—Mr. Ras Lal," said Ram, with whom the English language was not a strong point.

"Then he's a fool!" growled Tommy. "Gosh! he put my heart in my mouth!"

While Ram was getting together sufficient English to explain what had happened, Tommy passed on. He found his client sitting in the lobby, a black cheroot between his teeth, a smile of satisfaction on his dark face.

"Welcome!" he said, as Tommy closed the door. "We have trapped the weasel."

"Never mind about the weasel," said the other impatiently. "Did you find the rupees?"

Ras Lal shook his head.

"But I left them in the store—ten thousand notes. I thought you'd have got them and skipped before this," said Mr. Fenalow anxiously.

"I have something more important in the store—come and see my friend."

He preceded the bewildered Tommy up the stairs, turned on the landing light and threw open the door.

"Behold——" he said, and said no more.

"Why, it is Mr. Fenalow!" said Mr. J. G.

One hand held a packet of almost life-like rupee notes; as for the other hand——

"You oughter known he carried a gun, you dam' black baboon," hissed Tommy. "An' to put him in a room where the stuff was, *and* a telephone!"

He was being driven to the local police station, and for the moment was attached to his companion by links of steel.

"It was a mere jest or a piece of practical joking, as I shall explain to the judge in the morning," said Ras airily.

Tommy Fenalow's reply was unprintable.

*   *   *   *   *

Three o'clock boomed out from St. John's Church as Mr. Reeder accompanied an excited girl to the front door of her boardinghouse.

"I can't tell you how I—I've enjoyed tonight," she said.

Mr. Reeder glanced uneasily at the dark face of the house.

"I hope—er—your friends will not think it remarkable that you should return at such an hour."

Despite her assurance, he went slowly home with an uneasy feeling that her name had in some way been compromised. And in melodrama, when a heroine's name is compromised, somebody has to marry her.

That was the disturbing thought that kept Mr. Reeder awake all night.

VI

The Green Mamba

The spirit of exploration for easy money has ruined more promising careers than drink, gambling, or the smiles of women. Generally speaking, the beaten tracks of life are the safest, and few men have adventured into the uncharted spaces in search of easy fortune who have not regarded the rediscovery of the old hard road whence they strayed as the greatest of their achievements.

Mo Liski held an assured position in his world, and one acquired by the strenuous and even violent exercise of his many qualities. He might have gone on until the end of the chapter, only he fell for an outside proposition, and, moreover, handicapped himself with a private feud, which had its beginning in an affair wholly remote from his normal operations.

There was a Moorish grafter named El Rahbut, who had made several visits to England, travelling by the banana boats which make the round trip from London River to Funchal Bay, Las Palmas, Tangier, and Oporto. He was a very ordinary, yellow-faced Moor, pock-marked and undersized, and he spoke English, having in his youth fallen into the hands of a well-meaning American missionary. This man Rahbut was useful to Mo because quite a lot of German drugs are shipped via Trieste to the Levant, and many a crate of oranges has been landed in the Pool that had, squeezed in their golden interiors, little metal cylinders containing smuggled heroin, cocaine, hydrochlorate, and divers other noxious medicaments.

Rahbut brought such things from time to time, was paid fairly and was satisfied. One day, in the saloon bar of The Four Jolly Seamen, he told Mo of a great steal. It had been carried out by a group of Anghera thieves working in Fez, and the loot was no less than the Emeralds of Suliman, the most treasured possession of Morocco. Not even Abdul Aziz in his most impecunious days had dared to remove them from the Mosque of Omar; the Anghera men being what they were, broke into the holy house, killed two guardians of the treasure, and had got away with the nine green stones of the great king. Thereafter arose an outcry which was heard from the bazars of Calcutta to the mean streets of Marsi-Karsi. But the men of Anghera were superior to the voice of public opinion and they did no more than seek

70

a buyer. El Rahbut, being a notorious bad character, came into the matter, and this was the tale he told to Mo Liski at The Four Jolly Seamen one foggy October night.

"There is a million pesetas' profit in this for you and me, Mr. Good Man," said Rahbut (all Europeans who paid on the nail were "Mr. Good Man" to El Rahbut). "There is also death for me if this thing becomes known."

Mo listened, smoothing his chin with a hand that sparkled and flashed dazzlingly. He was keen on ornamentation. It was a little outside his line, but the newspapers had stated the bald value of the stolen property, and his blood was on fire at the prospect of earning half a million so easily. That Scotland Yard and every police headquarters in the world were on the look-out for the nine stones of Suliman did not greatly disturb him. He knew the subterranean way down which a polished stone might slide; and if the worst came to the worst, there was a reward of £5,000 for the recovery of the jewels.

"I'll think it over; where is the stuff?"

"Here," said Rahbut, to the other's surprise. "In ten-twenty minutes I could lay them on your hands, Mr. Good Man."

Here seemed a straightforward piece of negotiation; it was doubly unfortunate that at that very period he should find himself mixed up in an affair which promised no profit whatever—the feud of Marylou Plessy, which was to become his because of his high regard for the lady.

When a woman is bad, she is usually very bad indeed, and Marylou Plessy was an extremely malignant woman. She was rather tall and handsome, with black sleek hair, boyishly shingled, and a heavy black fringe that covered a forehead of some distinction.

Mr. Reeder saw her once: he was at the Central Criminal Court giving evidence against Bartholomew Xavier Plessy, an ingenious Frenchman who had discovered a new way of making old money. His forgeries were well-nigh undetectable, but Mr. Reeder was no ordinary man. He not only detected them, but he traced the printer, and that was why Bartholomew Xavier faced an unimpassioned judge, who told him in a hushed voice how very wrong it was to debase the currency; how it struck at the very roots of our commercial and industrial life. This the debonair man in the dock did not resent. He knew all about it. It was the judge's curt postscript which made him wince.

"You will be kept in penal servitude for twenty years."

That Marylou loved the man is open to question. The probabilities are that she did not; but she hated Mr. Reeder, and she hated him not because he had brought her man to his undoing, but because, in the course of his evidence, he had used the phrase "the woman with whom the prisoner is associated." And Mr. John Reeder could have put her beside Plessy in the dock had he so wished: she knew this too and loathed him for his mercifulness.

Mrs. Plessy had a large flat in Portland Street. It was in a block which was the joint property of herself and her husband, for their graft had been on the grand scale, and Mr. Plessy owned race-horses before he owned a number in Parkhurst Convict Establishment. And here Marylou entertained lavishly.

A few months after her husband went to prison, she dined *tête-à-tête* with Mo Liski, the biggest of the gang leaders and an uncrowned emperor of the underworld. He was a small, dapper man who wore pince-nez and looked rather like a member of one of the learned professions. Yet he ruled the Strafas and the Sullivans and the Birklows, and his word was law on a dozen race-tracks, in a score of spieling clubs and innumerable establishments less liable to police supervision. People opposing him were incontinently "coshed"—rival leaders more or less paid tribute and walked warily at that. He levied toll upon bookmakers and was immune from police interference by reason of their two failures to convict him.

Since there are white specks on the blackest coat, he had this redeeming feature, that Marylou Plessy was his ideal woman, and it is creditable in a thief to possess ideals, however unworthily they may be disposed.

He listened intently to Marylou's views, playing with his thin watchguard, his eyes on the embroidery of the tablecloth. But though he loved her, his native caution held him to reason.

"That's all right, Marylou," he said. "I dare say I could get Reeder, but what is going to happen then? There will be a squeak louder than a bus brake! And he's dangerous. I never worry about the regular busies, but this old feller is in the Public Prosecutor's office, and he wasn't put there because he's silly. And just now I've got one of the biggest deals on that I've ever touched. Can't you do him yourself? You're a clever woman: I don't know a cleverer."

"Of course, if you're scared of Reeder——!" she said contemptuously, and a tolerant smile twisted his thin lips.

"Me? Don't be silly, dearie! Show him a point yourself. If you can't get him, let me know. Scared of him! Listen! That old bird would lose his feathers and be skinned for the pot before you could say 'Mo Liski' if I wanted!"

In the Public Prosecutor's office they had no doubt about Mr. Reeder's ability to take care of himself, and when Chief Inspector Pyne came over from the Yard to report that Marylou had been in conference with the most dangerous man in London, the Assistant Prosecutor grinned his amusement.

"No—Reeder wants no protection. I'll tell him if you like, but he probably knows all about it. What are you people doing about the Liski crowd?"

Pyne pulled a long face.

"We've had Liski twice, but well-organized perjury has saved him. The Assistant Commissioner doesn't want him again till we get him with the blood on his hands, so to speak. He's dangerous."

The Assistant Prosecutor nodded.

"So is Reeder," he said ominously. "That man is a genial *mamba*! Never seen a *mamba*? He's a nice black snake, and you're dead two seconds after he strikes!"

The chief inspector's smile was one of incredulity.

"He never impressed me that way—rabbit, yes, but snake, no!"

Later in the morning a messenger brought Mr. Reeder to the chief's office, and he arrived with that ineffable air of apology and diffidence which gave the uninitiated such an altogether wrong idea of his calibre. He listened with closed eyes whilst his superior told him of the meeting between Liski and Marylou.

"Yes, sir," he sighed, when the narrative came to an end. "I have heard rumours. Liski? He is the person who associates with unlawful characters? In other days and under more favourable conditions he would have been the leader of a Florentine faction. An interesting man. With interesting friends."

"I hope your interest remains impersonal," warned the lawyer, and Mr. Reeder sighed again, opened his mouth to speak, hesitated, and then:

"Doesn't the continued freedom of Mr. Liski cast—um—a reflection upon our department, sir?" he asked.

His chief looked up: it was an inspiration which made him say:

"Get him!"

Mr. Reeder nodded very slowly.

"I have often thought that it would be a good idea," he said. His gaze deepened in melancholy. "Liski has many acquaintances of a curious character," he said at last. "Dutchmen, Russians, Jewish persons—he knows a Moor."

The chief looked up quickly.

"A Moor—you're thinking of the Nine Emeralds? My dear man, there are hundreds of Moors in London and thousands in Paris."

"And millions in Morocco," murmured Mr. Reeder. "I only mention the Moor in passing, sir. As regards my friend Mrs. Plessy—I hope only for the best."

And he melted from the room.

The greater part of a month passed before he showed any apparent interest in the case. He spent odd hours wandering in the neighbourhood of Lambeth, and on one occasion he was seen in the members' enclosure at Hurst Park race-track—but he spoke to nobody, and nobody spoke to him.

One night Mr. Reeder came dreamily back to his well-ordered house in Brockley Road, and found waiting on his table a small flat box which had arrived, his housekeeper told him, by post that afternoon. The label was addressed in typewritten characters "John Reeder, Esq.," and the postmark was Central London.

He cut the thin ribbon which tied it, stripped first the brown paper and then the silver tissue, and exposed a satiny lid, which he lifted daintily. There, under a layer of paper shavings, were roll upon roll of luscious confectionery. Chocolate, with or without dainty extras, had an appeal for Mr. Reeder, and he took up a small globule garnished with crystallised violets and examined it admiringly.

His housekeeper came in at that moment with his tea-tray and set it down on the table. Mr. Reeder looked over his large glasses.

"Do you like chocolates, Mrs. Kerrel?" he asked plaintively.

"Why, yes, sir," the elderly lady beamed.

"So do I," said Mr. Reeder. "So do I!" and he shook his head regretfully, as he replaced the chocolate carefully in the box. "Unfortunately," he went on, "my doctor—a very excellent man—has forbidden me all sorts of confectionery until they have been submitted to the rigorous test of the public analyst."

Mrs. Kerrel was a slow thinker, but a study of current advertisement columns in the daily newspaper had enlarged to a very considerable extent her scientific knowledge.

"To see if there is any vitamines in them, sir?" she suggested.

Mr. Reeder shook his head.

"No, I hardly think so," he said gently. "Vitamines are my sole diet. I can spend a whole evening with no other company than a pair of these interesting little fellows, and take no ill from them. Thank you, Mrs. Kerrel."

When she had gone, he replaced the layer of shavings with punctilious care, closed down the lid, and as carefully re-wrapped the parcel. When it was finished he addressed the package to a department at Scotland Yard, took from a small box a label printed redly "Poison." When this was done, he scribbled a note to the gentleman affected, and addressed himself to his muffins and his large teacup.

It was a quarter past six in the evening when he had unwrapped the chocolates. It was exactly a quarter past eleven, as he turned out the lights preparatory to going to bed, that he said aloud:

"Marylou Plessy—dear me!"

Here began the war.

This was Wednesday evening; on Friday morning the toilet of Marylou Plessy was interrupted by the arrival of two men who were waiting for her when she came into the sitting room in her *négligé*. They talked about finger prints found on chocolates and other such matters.

Half an hour later a dazed woman sat in the cells at Harlboro Street and listened to an inspector's recital of her offence. At the following sessions she went down for two years on a charge of "conveying by post to John Reeder a poisonous substance, to wit aconitine, with intent to murder."

To the last Mo Liski sat in court, his drawn, haggard face testifying to the strength of his affection for the woman in the dock. After she disappeared from the dock he went outside into the big, windy hall, and there and then made his first mistake.

Mr. Reeder was putting on his woollen gloves when the dapper man strode up to him.

"Name of Reeder?"

"That is my name, sir."

Mr. Reeder surveyed him benevolently over his glasses. He had the expectant air of one who has steeled himself to receive congratulations.

"Mine is Mo Liski. You've sent down a friend of mine——"

"Mrs. Plessy?"

"Yes—you know! Reeder, I'm going to get you for that!"

Instantly somebody behind him caught his arm in a vise and swung him round. It was a city detective.

"Take a walk with me," he said.

Mo went white. Remember that he owed the strength of his position to the fact that never once had he been convicted: the register did not bear his name.

"What's the charge?" he asked huskily.

"Intimidation of a Crown witness and using threatening language," said the officer.

Mo came up before the Aldermen at the Guildhall the next morning and was sent to prison for three weeks, and Mr. Reeder, who knew the threat would come and was ready to counter with the traditional swiftness of the mamba, felt that he had scored a point. The gang leader was, in the parlance of the law, "a convicted person."

"I don't think anything will happen until he comes out," he said to Pyne, when he was offered police protection. "He will find a great deal of

satisfaction in arranging the details of my—um—bashing, and I feel sure
that he will postpone action until he is free. I had better have that protection
until he comes out——"

"After he comes out, you mean?"

"*Until* he comes out," insisted Mr. Reeder carefully. "After—well—
um—I'd rather like to be unhampered by—um—police protection."

Mo Liski came to his liberty with all his senses alert. The cat-caution
which had, with only one break, kept him clear of trouble, dominated his
every plan. Cold-bloodedly he cursed himself for jeopardising his emerald
deal, and his first step was to get into touch with El Rahbut.

But there was a maddening new factor in his life: the bitter consciousness
of his fallibility and the fear that the men he had ruled so completely might,
in consequence, attempt to break away from their allegiance. There was
something more than sentiment behind this fear. Mo drew close on fifteen
thousand a year from his race-course and club-house victims alone. There
were pickings on the side: his "crowd" largely controlled a continental
drug traffic worth thousands a year. Which may read romantic and imagi-
native, but was true. Not all the "bunce" came to Mo and his men. There
were pickings for the carrion fowl as well as for the wolves.

He must fix Reeder. That was the first move. And fix him so that there
was no recoil. To beat him up one night would be an easy matter, but that
would look too much like carrying into execution the threat which had put
him behind bars. Obviously some ingenuity was called for; some exquisite
punishment more poignant than the shock of clubs.

Men of Mr. Liski's peculiar calling do not meet their lieutenants in dark
cellars, nor do they wear cloaks or masks to disguise their identities. The
big six who controlled the interests serving Mo Liski came together on the
night of his release, and the gathering was at a Soho restaurant, where a
private dining-room was engaged in the ordinary way.

"I'm glad nobody touched him while I was away," said Mo with a little
smile. "I'd like to manage this game myself. I've been doing some thinking
while I was in bird, and there's a good way to deal with him."

"He had two coppers with him all the time, or I'd have coshed him for
you, Mo," said Teddy Alfield, his chief of staff.

"And I'd have coshed you, Teddy," said Mr. Liski ominously. "I left
orders that he wasn't to be touched, didn't I? What do you mean by you'd
'have coshed him'?"

Alfield, a big-shouldered man whose specialty was the "knocking-off" of
unattended motor cars, grew incoherent.

"You stick to your job," snarled Mo. "I'll fix Reeder. He's got a girl in
Brockley; a young woman who is always going about with him—Belman's

her name and she lives nearly opposite his house. We don't want to beat him up—yet. What we want to do is to get him out of his job, and that's easy. They fired a man in the Home Office last week because he was found at the '95' Club after drinking hours.''

He outlined a simple plan.

Margaret Belman left her office one evening and, walking to the corner of Westminster Bridge and the Embankment, looked around for Mr. Reeder. Usually, if his business permitted, he was to be found hereabouts, though of late the meetings had been very few, and when she had seen him he was usually in the company of two glum men who seated themselves on either side of him.

She let one car pass, and had decided to catch the second which was coming slowly along the Embankment, when a parcel dropped at her feet. She looked round to see a pretty, well-dressed woman swaying with closed eyes, and had just time to catch her by the arm before she half collapsed. With her arm round the woman's waist she assisted her to a seat providentially placed hereabouts.

"I'm so sorry—thank you ever so much. I wonder if you would call me a taxi?'' gasped the fainting lady.

She spoke with a slightly foreign accent, and had the indefinable manner of a great lady; so Margaret thought.

Beckoning a cab, she assisted the woman to enter.

"Would you like me to go home with you?'' asked the sympathetic girl.

"It would be good of you,'' murmured the lady, "but I fear to inconvenience you—it was so silly of me. My address is 105 Great Claridge Street.''

She recovered sufficiently on the journey to tell Margaret that she was Madame Lemaire, and that she was the widow of a French banker. The beautiful appointments of the big house in the most fashionable part of Mayfair suggested that Madame Lemaire was a woman of some wealth. A butler opened the door, a liveried footman brought in the tea which Madame insisted on the girl having with her.

"You are too good. I cannot be thankful enough to you, mademoiselle. I must know you better. Will you come one night to dinner? Shall we say Thursday?''

Margaret Belman hesitated. She was human enough to be impressed by the luxury of her surroundings, and this dainty lady had the appeal of refinement and charm which is so difficult to resist.

"We will dine *tête-à-tête*, and after—some people may come for dancing. Perhaps you have a friend who would like to come?''

Margaret smiled and shook her head. Curiously enough, the word "friend" suggested only the rather awkward figure of Mr. Reeder, and somehow she could not imagine Mr. Reeder in this setting.

When she came out into the street and the butler had closed the door behind her, she had the first shock of the day. The object of her thoughts was standing on the opposite side of the road, a furled umbrella hooked to his arm.

"Why, Mr. Reeder!" she greeted him.

"You had seven minutes to spare," he said, looking at his big-faced watch. "I gave you half an hour—you were exactly twenty-three minutes and a few odd seconds."

"Did you know I was there?" she asked unnecessarily.

"Yes—I followed you. I do not like Mrs. Annie Feltham—she calls herself Madame something or other. It is not a nice club."

"Club!" she gasped.

Mr. Reeder nodded.

"They call it the Muffin Club. Curious name—curious members. It is not nice."

She asked no further questions, but allowed herself to be escorted to Brockley, wondering just why Madame had picked upon her as a likely recruit to the gaieties of Mayfair.

And now occurred the succession of incidents which at first had so puzzled Mr. Liski. He was a busy man, and almost regretted that he had not postponed putting his plan of operation into movement. That he had failed in one respect he discovered when by accident, as it seemed, he met Mr. Reeder face to face in Piccadilly.

"*Good*-morning, Liski," said Mr. Reeder, almost apologetically. "I was so sorry for that unfortunate contretemps, but believe me, I bear no malice. And while I realise that in all probability you do not share my sentiments, I have no other wish than to live on the friendliest terms with you."

Liski looked at him sharply. The old man was getting scared, he thought. There was almost a tremble in his anxious voice when he put forward the olive branch.

"That's all right, Mr. Reeder," said Mo, with his most charming smile. "I don't bear any malice either. After all, it was a silly thing to say, and you have your duty to do."

He went on in this strain, stringing platitude to platitude, and Mr. Reeder listened with evidence of growing relief.

"The world is full of sin and trouble," he said, shaking his head sadly; "both in high and low places vice is triumphant, and virtue thrust, like the daisies, underfoot. You don't keep chickens, do you, Mr. Liski?"

Mo Liski shook his head.

"What a pity!" sighed Mr. Reeder. "There is so much one can learn from the domestic fowl! They are an object lesson to the unlawful. I often wonder why the Prison Commissioners do not allow the convicts at Dartmoor to engage in this harmless and instructive hobby. I was saying to Mr. Pyne early this morning, when they raided the Muffin Club—what a quaint title it has——''

"Raided the Muffin Club?" said Mo quickly. "What do you mean? I've heard nothing about that."

"You wouldn't. That kind of institution would hardly appeal to you. Only we thought it was best to raid the place, though in doing so I fear I have incurred the displeasure of a young lady friend of mine who was invited to dinner there to-morrow night. As I say, chickens——''

Now Mo Liski knew that his plan had miscarried. Yet he was puzzled by the man's attitude.

"Perhaps you would like to come down and see my Buff Orpingtons, Mr. Liski? I live in Brockley." Reeder removed his glasses and glared owlishly at his companion. "Say at nine o'clock to-night; there is so much to talk about. At the same time, it would add to the comfort of all concerned if you did not arrive—um—conspicuously: do you understand what I mean? I should not like the people of my office, for example, to know."

A slow smile dawned on Liski's face. It was his faith that all men had their price, whether it was paid in cash or terror; and this invitation to a secret conference was in a sense a tribute to the power he wielded.

At nine o'clock he came to Brockley, half hoping that Mr. Reeder would go a little farther along the road which leads to compromise. But, strangely enough, the elderly detective talked of nothing but chickens. He sat on one side of the table, his hands clasped on the cloth, his voice vibrant with pride as he spoke of the breed that he was introducing to the English fowl-house, and, bored to extinction, Mo waited.

"There is something I wanted to say to you, but I fear that I must postpone that until another meeting," said Mr. Reeder, as he helped his visitor on with his coat. "I will walk with you to the corner of Lewisham High Road: the place is full of bad characters, and I shouldn't like to feel that I had endangered your well-being by bringing you to this lowly spot."

Now, if there is one place in the world which is highly respectable and free from the footpads which infest wealthier neighbourhoods, it is Brockley Road. Liski submitted to the company of his host, and walked to the church at the end of the road.

"Good-bye, Mr. Liski," said Reeder earnestly. "I shall never forget this pleasant meeting. You have been of the greatest help and assistance to me. You may be sure that neither I nor the department I have the honour to represent will ever forget you."

Liski went back to town, a frankly bewildered man. In the early hours of the morning the police arrested his chief lieutenant, Teddy Alfield, and charged him with a motor-car robbery which had been committed three months before.

That was the first of the inexplicable happenings. The second came when Liski, returning to his flat off Portland Place, was suddenly confronted by the awkward figure of the detective.

"Is that Liski?" Mr. Reeder peered forward in the darkness. "I'm so glad I've found you. I've been looking for you all day. I fear I horribly misled you the other evening when I was telling you that Leghorns are unsuitable for sandy soil. Now on the contrary——"

"Look here, Mr. Reeder, what's the game?" demanded the other brusquely.

"The game?" asked Reeder in a pained tone.

"I don't want to know anything about chickens. If you've got anything to tell me worth while, drop me a line and I'll come to your office, or you can come to mine."

He brushed past the man from the Public Prosecutor's Department and slammed the door of his flat behind him. Within two hours a squad from Scotland Yard descended upon the house of Harry Merton, took Harry and his wife from their respective beds, and charged them with the unlawful possession of stolen jewellery which had been traced to a safe deposit.

A week later, Liski, returning from a vital interview with El Rahbut, heard plodding steps overtaking him, and turned to meet the pained eye of Mr. Reeder.

"How providential meeting you!" said Reeder fervently. "No, no, I do not wish to speak about chickens, though I am hurt a little by your indifference to this noble and productive bird."

"Then what in hell do you want?" snapped Liski. "I don't want anything to do with you, Reeder, and the sooner you get that into your system the better. I don't want to discuss fowls, horses——"

"Wait!" Mr. Reeder bent forward and lowered his voice. "Is it not possible for you and me to meet together and exchange confidences?"

Mo Liski smiled slowly.

"Oh, you're coming to it at last, eh? All right. I'll meet you anywhere you please."

"Shall we say in the Mall near the Artillery statue, to-morrow night at ten? I don't think we shall be seen there."

Liski nodded shortly and went on, still wondering what the man had to tell him. At four o'clock he was wakened by the telephone ringing furiously, and learnt, to his horror, that O'Hara, the most trustworthy of his gang leaders, had been arrested and charged with a year-old burglary. It was Carter, one of the minor leaders, who brought the news.

"What's the idea, Liski?" And there was a note of suspicion in the voice of his subordinate which made Liski's jaw drop.

"What do you mean—what's the idea? Come round and see me. I don't want to talk over the phone."

Carter arrived half an hour later, a scowling, suspicious man.

"Now what do you want to say?" asked Mo, when they were alone.

"All I've got to say is this," growled Carter: "a week ago you're seen talking to old Reeder in Lewisham Road, and the same night Teddy Alfield is pinched. You're spotted having a quiet talk with this old dog, and the same night another of the gang goes west. Last night I saw you with my own eyes having a confidential chat with Reeder—and now O'Hara's gone!"

Mo looked at him incredulously.

"Well, and what about it?" he asked.

"Nothing—except that it's a queer coincidence, that's all," said Carter, his lip curling. "The boys have been talking about it: they don't like it, and you can't blame them."

Liski sat pinching his lip, a far-away look in his eyes. It was true, though the coincidence had not struck him before. So that was the old devil's game! He was undermining his authority, arousing a wave of suspicion which, if it were not checked, would sweep him from his position.

"All right, Carter," he said, in a surprisingly mild tone. "It never hit me that way before. Now I'll tell you, and you can tell the other boys just what has happened."

In a few words he explained Mr. Reeder's invitations.

"And you can tell 'em from me that I'm meeting the old fellow to-morrow night, and I'm going to give him something to remember me by."

The thing was clear to him now as he sat, after the man's departure, going over the events of the past week. The three men who had been arrested had been under police suspicion for a long time, and Mo knew that not even he could have saved them. The arrests had been made by arrangement with Scotland Yard to suit the convenience of the artful Mr. Reeder.

"I'll 'artful' him!" said Mo, and spent the rest of the day making his preparations.

At ten o'clock that night he passed under the Admiralty Arch. A yellow mist covered the park, a drizzle of rain was falling, and save for the cars that came at odd intervals toward the palace, there was no sign of life.

He walked steadily past the Memorial, waiting for Mr. Reeder. Ten o'clock struck and a quarter past, but there was no sign of the detective.

"He's smelt a rat," said Mo Liski between his teeth, and replaced the short life-preserver he had carried in his pocket.

It was at eleven o'clock that a patrolling police-constable fell over a groaning something that lay across the sidewalk, and, flashing his electric lamp upon the still figure, saw the carved handle of a Moorish knife before he recognised the pain-distorted face of the stricken Mo Liski.

* * * * *

"I don't quite understand how it all came about," said Pyne thoughtfully. (He had been called into consultation from headquarters.) "Why are you so sure it was the Moor Rahbut?"

"I am not sure," Mr. Reeder hastened to correct the mistaken impression. "I mentioned Rahbut because I had seen him in the afternoon and searched his lodgings for the emeralds—which I am perfectly sure are still in Morocco, sir." He addressed his chief. "Mr. Rahbut was quite a reasonable man, remembering that he is a stranger to our methods."

"Did you mention Mo Liski at all, Mr. Reeder?" asked the Assistant Public Prosecutor.

Mr. Reeder scratched his chin.

"I think I did—yes, I'm pretty certain that I told him that I had an appointment with Mr. Liski at ten o'clock. I may even have said where the appointment was to be kept. I can't remember exactly how the subject of Liski came up. Possibly I may have tried to bluff this indigenous native—'bluff' is a vulgar word, but it will convey what I mean—into the belief that unless he gave me more information about the emeralds, I should be compelled to consult one who knew so many secrets. Possibly I did say that. Mr. Liski will be a long time in hospital, I hear? That is a pity. I should never forgive myself if my incautious words resulted in poor Mr. Liski being taken to the hospital—alive!"

When he had gone, the chief looked at Inspector Pyne.

Pyne smiled.

"What is the name of that dangerous reptile, sir?" asked the inspector. "'Mamba,' isn't it? I must remember that."

VII

The Strange Case

In the days of Mr. Reeder's youth, which were also the days when hansom cabs plied for hire and no gentleman went abroad without a nosegay in the lapel of his coat, he had been sent, in company with another young officer from Scotland Yard, to arrest a youthful inventor of Nottingham who earned more than a competence by methods which were displeasing to Scotland Yard. Not machines nor ingenious contrivances for saving labour did this young man invent—but stories. And they were not stories in the accepted sense of the word, for they were misstatements designed to extract money from the pockets of simpleminded men and women. Mr. Elter employed no fewer than twenty-five aliases and as many addresses in the broadcasting of his fiction, and he was on the way to amassing a considerable fortune when a square-toed Nemesis took him by the arm and led him to the seat of justice. An unsympathetic judge sent Mr. Elter to seven years' penal servitude, describing him as an unconscionable swindler and a menace to society—at which Willie Elter smiled, for he had a skin beside which the elephant's was gossamer silk.

Mr. Reeder remembered the case chiefly because the prosecuting attorney, commenting upon the various disguises and subterfuges which the prisoner had adopted, remarked upon a peculiarity which was revealed in every part which the convict had played—his inability to spell "able," which he invariably wrote as though he were naming the victim of Cain's envy.

"There is this identity to be discovered in every criminal, however ingenious he may be," the advocate had said. "Whatever his disguise, no matter how cleverly he dissociates one rôle or pose from another, there is a distinguishable weakness common to every character he affects, and especially is this observable in criminals who live by fraud and trickery."

This Mr. Reeder remembered throughout his useful life. Few people knew that he had ever been associated with Scotland Yard. He himself evaded any question that was put to him on the subject. It was his amiable trait to pretend that he was the veriest amateur and that his success in the detection of wrongdoing was to be traced to his own evil mind that saw wrong very often where no wrong was.

He saw wrong in so many apparently innocent acts of man that it was well for his reputation that those who were acquainted with and pitied him because of his seeming inadequacy and unattractive appearance did not know what dark thoughts filled his mind.

There was a very pretty girl who lived in Brockley Road at a boarding-house. He did not like Miss Margaret Belman because she was pretty, but because she was sensible: two terms which are as a rule antagonistic. He liked her so well that he often travelled home on the cars with her, and they used to discuss the Prince of Wales, the Labour Government, the high cost of living, and other tender subjects with great animation. It was from Miss Belman that he learned about her fellow-boarder, Mrs. Carlin, and once he travelled back with her to Brockley—a frail, slim girl with experience in her face and the hint of tragedy in her fine eyes.

So it happened that he knew all about Mr. Harry Carlin long before Lord Sellington sent for him, for Mr. Reeder had the gift of evoking confidences by the suggestion rather than the expression of his sympathy.

She spoke of her husband without bitterness—but also without regret. She knew him rather well, despite the shortness of their married life. She hinted once and inadvertently, that there was a rich relation to whose wealth her husband would be heir if he were a normal man. Her son would, in due course, be the possessor of a great title—and penniless. She was at such pains to rectify her statement that Mr. Reeder, suspicious of peerages that come to Brockley, was assured of her sincerity, however great might be her error. Later he learned that the title was that borne by the Right Honourable the Earl of Sellington and Manford.

There came a slack time for the Public Prosecutor's office, when it seemed that sin had gone out of the world; and Mr. Reeder sat for a week on end in his little room, twiddling his thumbs or reading the advertisement columns of *The Times*, or drawing grotesque men upon his blotting-pad, varying these performances with the excursions he was in the habit of making to those parts of London which very few people choose for their recreation. He loved to poke about the slum areas which lie in the neighbourhood of the Great Surrey Docks; he was not averse from frequenting the north side of the river, again in the dock areas; but when his chief asked him whether he spent much time at Limehouse, Mr. Reeder replied with a pathetic smile.

"No, sir," he said gently, "I read about such places—I find them infinitely more interesting in the pages of a—er—novel. Yes, there are Chinese there, and I suppose Chinese are romantic, but even they do not add romance to Limehouse, which is the most respectable and law-abiding corner of the East End.''

One morning the Public Prosecutor sent for his chief detective, and Mr. Reeder obeyed the summons with a light step and a pleasant sense of anticipation.

''Go over to the Foreign Office and have a talk with Lord Sellington,'' said the Prosecutor. ''He is rather worried about a nephew of his, Harry Carlin. Do you know the name?''

Mr. Reeder shook his head; for the moment he did not associate the pale girl who typed for her living.

''He's a pretty bad lot,'' explained the Prosecutor, ''and unfortunately he's Sellington's heir. I rather imagine the old gentleman wants you to confirm his view.''

''Dear me!'' said Mr. Reeder, and stole forth.

Lord Sellington, Under-Secretary of State for Foreign Affairs, was a bachelor and an immensely rich man. He had been rich in 1912, when, in a panic due to certain legislation which he thought would affect him adversely as a great landowner, he sold his estates and invested the larger bulk of his fortune (against all expert advice) in American industrial stocks. The war had trebled his possessions. Heavy investments in oil lands had made him many times a millionaire. He was a philanthropist, gave liberally to institutions devoted to the care of young children; he was the founder of the Eastleigh Children's Home, and subscribed liberally to other similar institutions. A thin, rather sour-faced man, he glared up under his shaggy eyebrows as Mr. Reeder sidled apologetically into his room.

''So you're Reeder, eh?'' he grumbled, and was evidently not very much impressed by his visitor. 'Sit down, sit down,'' he said testily, walked to the door as though he were not certain that Mr. Reeder had closed it, and came back and flopped into his chair on the other side of the table. ''I have sent for you in preference to notifying the police,'' he said. ''Sir James speaks of you, Mr. Reeder, as a gentleman of discretion.''

Mr. Reeder bowed slightly, and there followed a long and awkward pause, which the Under-Secretary ended in an abrupt, irritable way.

''I have a nephew—Harry Carlin. Do you know him?''

''I know of him,'' said Mr. Reeder truthfully; in his walk to the Foreign Office he had remembered the deserted wife.

''Then you know nothing good of him!'' exploded his lordship. ''The man is a blackguard, a waster, a disgrace to the name he bears! If he were not my brother's son I would have him under lock and key to-night—the scoundrel! I have four bills in my possession——''

He stopped himself, pulled open a drawer savagely, took out a letter and slammed it on the table.

"Read that," he snapped.

Mr. Reeder pulled his glasses a little farther up his nose (he always held them very tight when he was really using them) and perused the message. It was headed "The Eastleigh Home for Children," and was a brief request for five thousand pounds, which the writer said he would send for that evening, and was signed "Arthur Lassard."

"You know Lassard, of course?" said his lordship. "He is the gentleman associated with me in my philanthropic work. Certain monies were due for land which we purchased adjoining the home. As you probably know, there are lawyers who never accept checks for properties they sell on behalf of their clients, and I had the money ready and left it with my secretary, and one of Lassard's people was calling for it. That it was called for, I need hardly tell you," said his lordship grimly. "Whoever planned the coup planned it well. They knew I would be speaking in the House of Lords last night; they also knew that I had recently changed my secretary and had engaged a gentleman to whom most of my associates are strangers. A bearded man came for the money at half-past six, produced a note from Mr. Lassard, and that was the end of the money, except that we have discovered that it was changed this morning into American bills. Of course, both letters were forged: Lassard never signed either, and made no demand whatever for the money, which was not needed for another week."

"Did anybody know about this transaction?" asked Mr. Reeder.

His lordship nodded slowly.

"My nephew knew. He came to my house two days ago to borrow money. He has a small income from his late mother's estate, but insufficient to support him in his reckless extravagance. He admitted frankly to me that he had come back from Aix broke. How long he had been in London I am unable to tell you, but he was in my library when my secretary came in with the money which I had drawn from the bank in preparation for paying the bill when it became due. Very foolishly I explained why I had so much cash in the house and why I was unable to oblige him with the thousand pounds which he wanted to borrow," he added dourly.

Mr. Reeder scratched his chin.

"What am I to do?" he asked.

"I want you to find Carlin," Lord Sellington almost snarled. "But most I want that money back—you understand, Reeder? You're to tell him that unless he repays——"

Mr. Reeder was gazing steadily at the cornice moulding.

"It almost sounds as if I am being asked to compound a felony, my lord," he said respectfully. "But I realise, in the peculiar circumstances, we must adopt peculiar methods. The black-bearded gentleman who called for the money would appear to have been"—he hesitated—"disguised?"

"Of course he was disguised," said the other irritably.

"One reads of such things," said Mr. Reeder with a sigh, "but so seldom does the bearded stranger appear in real life! Will you be good enough to tell me your nephew's address?"

Lord Sellington took a card from his pocket and threw it across the table. It fell to the floor, but he did not apologise. He was that kind of man.

"Jermyn Mansions," said Mr. Reeder as he rose. "I will see what can be done."

Lord Sellington grunted something which might have been a tender farewell, but probably was not.

Jermyn Mansions is a very small, narrow-fronted building and, as Mr. Reeder knew—and he knew a great deal—was a block of residential flats, which were run by an ex-butler who was also the lessee of the establishment. By great good fortune, as he afterward learned, Harry Carlin was at home, and in a few minutes the man from the Public Prosecutor's office was ushered into a shabby drawing-room that overlooked Jermyn Street.

A tall young man stood by the window, looking disconsolately into that narrow and lively thoroughfare, and turned as Mr. Reeder was announced. Thin-faced, narrow-headed, small-eyed, if he possessed any of the family traits and failings, the most marked was perhaps his too ready irritation.

Mr. Reeder saw, through an open door, a very untidy bedroom, caught a glimpse of a battered trunk covered with continental labels.

"Well, what the devil do you want?" demanded Mr. Carlin. Yet, in spite of his tone, there was an undercurrent of disquiet which Mr. Reeder detected.

"May I sit down?" said the detective and, without waiting for an invitation, pulled a chair from the wall and sat down gingerly, for he knew the quality of lodging-house chairs.

His self-possession, the hint of authority he carried in his voice, increased Mr. Harry Carlin's uneasiness; and when Mr. Reeder plunged straight into the object of his visit, he saw the man go pale.

"It is a difficult subject to open," said Mr. Reeder, carefully smoothing his knees, "and when I find myself in that predicament I usually employ the plainest language."

And plain language he employed with a vengeance. Halfway through, Carlin sat down with a gasp.

"What—what!" he stammered. "Does that old brute dare——! I thought you came about the bills—I mean——"

"*I* mean," said Mr. Reeder carefully, "that if you have had a little fun with your relative, I think that jest has gone far enough. Lord Sellington is prepared, on the money being refunded, to regard the whole thing as an over-elaborate practical joke on your part——"

"But I haven't touched his beastly money!" the young man almost screamed. "I don't want his money——"

"On the contrary, sir," said Reeder gently, "you want it very badly. You left the Hotel Continental without paying your bill; you owe some six hundred pounds to various gentlemen from whom you borrowed that amount; there is a warrant out for you in France for passing checks which are usually described by the vulgar as—er—'dud.' Indeed"—again Mr. Reeder scratched his chin and looked thoughtfully out of the window—"indeed, I know no gentleman in Jermyn Street who is so badly in need of money as your good self."

Carlin would have stopped him, but the middle-aged man went on remorselessly.

"I have been for an hour in the Record Department of Scotland Yard, where your name is not unknown, Mr. Carlin. You left London rather hurriedly to avoid—er—proceedings of an unpleasant character. 'Bills,' I think you said? You are known to have been the associate of people with whom the police are a little better acquainted than they are with Mr. Carlin. You were also associated with a race-course fraud of a peculiarly unpleasant character. And amongst your minor delinquencies there is—er —a deserted young wife, at present engaged in a city office as a typist, and a small boy for whom you have never provided."

Carlin licked his dry lips.

"Is that all?" he asked, with an attempt at a sneer, though his voice shook and his trembling hands betrayed his agitation.

Reeder nodded.

"Well, I'll tell you something. I want to do the right thing by my wife. I admit I haven't played square with her, but I've never had the money to play square. That old devil has always been rolling in it, curse him! I'm the only relation he has, and what has he done? Left every bean to these damned children's homes of his! If somebody has caught him for five thousand I'm glad! I shouldn't have the nerve to do it myself, but I'm glad if they did —whoever they may be. Left every penny to a lot of squalling, sticky-faced brats, and not a bean to me!"

Mr. Reeder let him rave on without interruption, until at last, almost exhausted by his effort, he dropped down into a deep chair and glared at his visitor.

"Tell him that," he said breathlessly; "tell him that!"

Mr. Reeder made time to call at the little office in Portugal Street

wherein was housed the headquarters of Lord Sellington's various philanthropic enterprises. Mr. Arthur Lassard had evidently been in communica-
tion with his noble patron, for no sooner did Reeder give his name than he
was ushered into the plainly furnished room where the superintendent sat.

It was not unnatural that Lord Sellington should have as his assistant in
the good work so famous an organiser as Mr. Arthur Lassard. Mr.
Lassard's activities in the philanthropic world were many. A broad-
shouldered man with a jolly red face and a bald head, he had survived all
the attacks which come the way of men engaged in charitable work, and
was not particularly impressed by a recent visit he had had from Harry
Carlin.

"I don't wish to be unkind," he said, "but our friend called here on such
a lame excuse that I can't help feeling that his real object was to secure a
sheet of my stationery. I did, in fact, leave him in the room for a few
minutes, and he had the opportunity to purloin the paper if he desired."

"What was his excuse?" asked Mr. Reeder, and the other shrugged.

"He wanted money. At first he was civil and asked me to persuade his
uncle; then he grew abusive, said that I was conspiring to rob him—I and
my 'infernal charities'!"

He chuckled, but grew grave again.

"The situation is mysterious to me," he said. "Evidently Carlin has
committed some crime against his lordship, for he is terrified of him!"

"You think Mr. Carlin forged your name and secured the money?"

The superintendent spread out his arms in despair.

"Whom else can I suspect?" he asked.

Mr. Reeder took the forged letter from his pocket and read it again.

"I've just been on the 'phone to his lordship," Mr. Lassard went on.
"He is waiting, of course, to hear your report, and if you have failed to
make this young man confess his guilt, Lord Sellington intends seeing his
nephew to-night and making an appeal to him. I can hardly believe that
Mr. Carlin could have done this wicked thing, though the circumstances
seem very suspicious. Have you seen him, Mr. Reeder?"

"I have seen him," said Mr. Reeder shortly. "Oh, yes, I have seen
him!"

Mr. Arthur Lassard was scrutinising his face as though he were trying to
read the conclusion which the detective had reached, but Mr. Reeder's face
was notoriously expressionless.

He offered a limp hand and went back to the Under-Secretary's house.
The interview was short and on the whole disagreeable.

"I never dreamt he would confess to you," said Lord Sellington with ill-
disguised contempt. "Harry needs somebody to frighten him, and, my

God! I'm the man to do it! I'm seeing him to-night."

A fit of coughing stopped him and he gulped savagely from a little medicine bottle that stood on his desk.

"I'll see him to-night," he gasped, "and I'll tell him what I intend doing! I've spared him hitherto because of his relationship and because he inherits the title. But I'm through. Every cent I have goes to charity. I'm good for twenty years yet, but every penny——"

He stopped. He was a man who never disguised his emotion, and Mr. Reeder, who understood men, saw the struggle that was going on in Sellington's mind.

"He says he hasn't had a chance. I may have treated him unfairly—we shall see."

He waved the detective from his office as though he were dismissing a strange dog that had intruded upon his privacy, and Mr. Reeder went out reluctantly, for he had something to tell his lordship.

It was peculiar to him that, in his more secretive moments, he sought the privacy of his old-fashioned study in Brockley Road. For two hours he sat at his desk calling a succession of numbers—and curiously enough, the gentlemen to whom he spoke were bookmakers. Most of them he knew. In the days when he was the greatest expert in the world on forged currency notes, he had been brought into contact with a class which is often the innocent medium by which the forger distributed his handicraft—and more often the instrument of his detection.

It was a Friday, a day on which most of the principals were in their offices till a late hour. At eight o'clock he finished, wrote a note and, 'phoning for a messenger, sent his letter on its fateful errand.

He spent the rest of the evening musing on past experiences and in refreshing his memory from the thin scrap-books which filled two shelves in his study.

What happened elsewhere that evening can best be told in the plain language of the witness box. Lord Sellington had gone home after his interview with Mr. Reeder suffering from a feverish cold, and was disposed, according to the evidence of his secretary, to put off the interview which he had arranged with his nephew. A telephone message had been sent through to Mr. Carlin's hotel, but he was out. Until nine o'clock his lordship was busy with the affairs of his numerous charities, Mr. Lassard being in attendance. Lord Sellington was working in a small study which opened from his bedroom.

At a quarter past nine Carlin arrived and was shown upstairs by the butler, who subsequently stated that he heard voices raised in anger. Mr. Carlin came downstairs and was shown out as the clock struck half-past nine, and a few minutes later the bell rang for Lord Sellington's valet, who went up to assist his master to bed.

At half-past seven the next morning, the valet, who slept in an adjoining apartment, went into his master's room to take him a cup of tea. He found his employer lying face downward on the floor; he was dead, and had been dead for some hours. There was no sign of wounds, and at first glance it looked as though this man of sixty had collapsed in the night. But there were circumstances which pointed to some unusual happening. In Lord Sellington's bedroom was a small steel wall-safe, and the first thing the valet noticed was that this was open, papers were lying on the floor, and that in the grate was a heap of paper which, except for one corner, was entirely burnt.

The valet telephoned immediately for the doctor and for the police, and from that moment the case went out of Mr. Reeder's able hands.

Later that morning he reported briefly to his superior the result of his inquiries.

"Murder, I am afraid," he said sadly. "The Home Office pathologist is perfectly certain that it is a case of aconitine poisoning. The paper in the hearth has been photographed, and there is no doubt whatever that the burnt document is the will by which Lord Sellington left all his property to various charitable institutions."

He paused here.

"Well?" asked his chief, "what does that mean?"

Mr. Reeder coughed.

"It means that if this will cannot be proved, and I doubt whether it can, his lordship died intestate. The property goes with the title——"

"To Carlin?" asked the startled Prosecutor.

Mr. Reeder nodded.

"There were other things burnt; four small oblong slips of paper, which had evidently been fastened together by a pin. These are quite indecipherable." He sighed again. The Public Prosecutor looked up.

"You haven't mentioned the letter that arrived by district messenger after Lord Sellington had retired for the night."

Mr. Reeder rubbed his chin.

"No, I didn't mention that," he said reluctantly.

"Has it been found?"

Mr. Reeder hesitated.

"I don't know. I rather think that it has not been," he said.

"Would it throw any light upon the crime, do you think?"

Mr. Reeder scratched his chin with some sign of embarrassment.

"I should think it might," he said. "Will you excuse me, sir? Inspector

Salter is waiting for me.'' And he was out of the room before the Prosecutor could frame any further inquiry.

Inspector Salter was striding impatiently up and down the little room when Mr. Reeder came back. They left the building together. The car that was waiting for them brought them to Jermyn Street in a few minutes. Outside the flat three plain-clothes men were waiting, evidently for the arrival of their chief, and the Inspector passed into the building, followed closely by Mr. Reeder. They were half-way up the stairs when Reeder asked:

"Does Carlin know you?''

"He ought to,'' was the grim reply. "I did my best to get him penal servitude before he skipped from England.''

"Humph!'' said Mr. Reeder. "I'm sorry he knows you.''

"Why?'' The Inspector stopped on the stairs to ask the question.

"Because he saw us getting out of the cab. I caught sight of his face, and——''

He stopped suddenly. The sound of a shot thundered through the house, and in another second the Inspector was racing up the stairs two at a time and had burst into the suite which Carlin occupied.

A glimpse of the prostrate figure told them they were too late. The Inspector bent over the dead man.

"That has saved the country the cost of a murder trial,'' he said.

"I think not,'' said Mr. Reeder gently, and explained his reasons.

Half an hour later, as Mr. Lassard walked out of his office, a detective tapped him on the shoulder.

"Your name is Elter,'' he said, "and I want you for murder.''

*   *   *   *   *

"It was a very simple case really, sir,'' explained Mr. Reeder to his chief. "Elter, of course, was known to me personally, but I remembered especially that he could not spell the word 'able,' and I recognised this peculiarity in our friend the moment I saw the letter which he wrote to his patron asking for the money. It was Elter himself who drew the five thousand pounds; of that I am convinced. The man is, and always has been, an inveterate gambler, and I did not have to make many inquiries before I discovered that he was owing a large sum of money and that one bookmaker had threatened to bring him before Tattersall's Committee unless he paid. That would have meant the end of Mr. Lassard, the philanthropic custodian of children. Which, by the way, was always Elter's rôle. He ran bogus charitable societies—it is extraordinarily easy to find dupes who are willing to subscribe for philanthropic objects. Many years ago, when I was a young man, I was instrumental in getting him seven years. I'd lost sight of him since until I saw the letter he sent to Lord Sellington. Unfortunately for him, one line ran: 'I shall be glad if you are abel to let my messenger have the money'—and he spelt 'able' in the Elter way. I called on him and made sure. And then I wrote to his lordship, who apparently did not open the letter till late that night.

"Elter had called on him earlier in the evening and had had a long talk with him. I only surmise that Lord Sellington had expressed a doubt as to whether he ought to leave his nephew penniless, scoundrel though he was; and Elter was terrified that his scheme for getting possession of the old man's money was in danger of failing. Moreover, my appearance in the case had scared him. He decided to kill Lord Sellington that night, took aconitine with him to the house and introduced it into the medicine, a bottle of which always stood on Sellington's desk. Whether the old man destroyed the will which disinherited his nephew before he discovered he had been poisoned, or whether he did it after, we shall never know. When I had satisfied myself that Lassard was Elter, I sent a letter by special messenger to Stratford Place——"

"That was the letter delivered by special messenger?"

Mr. Reeder nodded.

"It is possible that Sellington was already under the influence of the drug when he burnt the will, and burnt too the four bills which Carlin had forged and which the old man had held over his head as a threat. Carlin may have known his uncle was dead; he certainly recognised the Inspector when he stepped out of the cab, and, thinking he was to be arrested for forgery, shot himself."

Mr. Reeder pursed his lips and his melancholy face grew longer.

"I wish I had never known Mrs. Carlin—my acquaintance with her introduces that element of coincidence which is permissible in stories but is so distressing in actual life. It shakes one's confidence in the logic of things."

VIII

The Investors

There are seven million people in Greater London and each one of those seven millions is in theory and practice equal under the law and commonly precious to the community. So that, if one is wilfully wronged, another must be punished; and if one dies of premeditated violence, his slayer must hang by the neck until he be dead.

It is rather difficult for the sharpest law-eyes to keep tag of seven million people, at least one million of whom never keep still and are generally unattached to any particular domicile. It is equally difficult to place an odd twenty thousand or so who have domiciles but no human association. These include tramps, aged maiden ladies in affluent circumstances, peripatetic members of the criminal classes, and other friendless individuals.

Sometimes uneasy inquiries come through to headquarters. Mainly they are most timid and deferential. Mr. X. has not seen his neighbour, Mr. Y., for a week. No, he doesn't know Mr. Y. Nobody does. A little old man who had no friends and spent his fine days pottering in a garden overlooked by his more gregarious neighbour. And now Mr. Y. potters no more. His milk has not been taken in; his blinds are drawn. Come a sergeant of police and a constable who break a window and climb through, and Mr. Y. is dead somewhere—dead of starvation or a fit of suicide. Should this be the case, all is plain sailing. But suppose the house empty and Mr. Y. disappeared. Here the situation becomes difficult and delicate.

Miss Elver went away to Switzerland. She was a middle-aged spinster who had the appearance of being comfortably circumstanced. She went away, locked up her house, and never came back. Switzerland looked for her; the myrmidons of Mussolini, that hatefully efficient man, searched North Italy from Domodossola to Montecatini. And the search did not yield a thin-faced maiden lady with a slight squint.

And then Mr. Charles Boyson Middlekirk, an eccentric and overpowering old man who quarrelled with his neighbours about their noisy children, he too went away. He told nobody where he was going. He lived alone with his three cats and was not on speaking terms with anybody else. He did not return to his grimy house.

He too was well off and reputedly a miser. So was Mrs. Athbell Marting, a dour widow who lived with her drudge of a niece. This lady was in the habit of disappearing without any preliminary announcement of her intention. The niece was allowed to order from the local tradesmen just sufficient food to keep body and soul together, and when Mrs. Marting returned (as she invariably did) the bills were settled with a great deal of grumbling on the part of the payer, and that was that. It was believed that Mrs. Marting went to Boulogne or to Paris or even to Brussels. But one day she went out and never came back. Six months later her niece advertised for her, choosing the cheapest papers—having an eye to the day of reckoning.

"Queer sort of thing," said the Public Prosecutor, who had before him the dossiers of four people (three women and a man) who had so vanished in three months.

He frowned, pressed a bell, and Mr. Reeder came in. Mr. Reeder took the chair that was indicated, looked owlishly over his glasses, and shook his head as though he understood the reason for his summons and denied his understanding in advance.

"What do you make of these disappearances?" asked his chief.

"You cannot make any positive of a negative," said Mr. Reeder carefully. "London is a large place full of strange, mad people who live such—um—commonplace lives that the wonder is that more of them do not disappear in order to do something different from what they are accustomed to doing."

"Have you seen these particulars?"

Mr. Reeder nodded.

"I have copies of them," he said. "Mr. Salter very kindly——"

The Public Prosecutor rubbed his head in perplexity.

"I see nothing in these cases—nothing in common, I mean. Four is a fairly low average for a big city——"

"Twenty-seven in twelve months," interrupted his detective apologetically.

"Twenty-seven—are you sure?" The great official was astounded.

Mr. Reeder nodded again.

"They were all people with a little money; all were drawing a fairly large income, which was paid to them in bank-notes on the first of every month—nineteen of them were, at any rate. I have yet to verify eight—and they were all most reticent as to where their revenues came from. None of them had any personal friends or relatives who were on terms of friendship, except Mrs. Marting. Beyond these points of resemblance there was nothing to connect one with the other."

The Prosecutor looked at him sharply, but Mr. Reeder was never sarcastic. Not obviously so, at any rate.

"There is another point which I omitted to mention," he went on. "After their disappearance no further money came for them. It came for Mrs. Marting when she was away on her jaunts, but it ceased when she went away on her final journey."

"But twenty-seven—are you sure?"

Mr. Reeder reeled off the list, giving name, address, and date of disappearance.

"What do you think has happened to them?"

Mr. Reeder considered for a moment, staring glumly at the carpet.

"I should imagine that they were murdered," he said, almost cheerfully, and the Prosecutor half rose from his chair.

"You are in your gayest mood this morning, Mr. Reeder," he said sardonically. "Why on earth should they be murdered?"

Mr. Reeder did not explain. The interview took place in the late afternoon, and he was anxious to be gone, for he had a tacit appointment to meet a young lady of exceeding charm who at five minutes after five would be waiting on the corner of Westminster Bridge and Thames Embankment for the Lee car.

The sentimental qualities of Mr. Reeder were entirely unknown. There are those who say that his sorrow over those whom fate and ill-fortune brought into his punitive hands was the veriest hypocrisy. There were others who believed that he was genuinely pained to see a fellow-creature sent behind bars through his efforts and evidence.

His housekeeper, who thought he was a woman-hater, told her friends in confidence that he was a complete stranger to the tender emotions which enlighten and glorify humanity. In the ten years which she had sacrificed to his service he had displayed neither emotion nor tenderness except to inquire whether her sciatica was better or to express a wish that she should take a holiday by the sea. She was a woman beyond middle age, but there is no period of life wherein a woman gives up hoping for the best. Though the most perfect of servants in all respects, she secretly despised him, called him, to her intimates, a frump, and suspected him of living apart from an ill-treated wife. This lady was a widow (as she had told him when he first engaged her) and she had seen better—far better—days.

Her visible attitude toward Mr. Reeder was one of respect and awe. She excused the queer character of his callers and his low acquaintances. She forgave him his square-toed shoes and high, flat-crowned hat, and even admired the ready-made Ascot cravat he wore and which was fastened behind the collar with a little buckle, the prongs of which invariably punctured his fingers when he fastened it. But there is a limit to all hero-worship, and when she discovered that Mr. Reeder was in the habit of waiting to escort a young lady to town every day, and frequently found it convenient to escort her home, the limit was reached.

Mrs. Hambleton told her friends—and they agreed—that there was no fool like an old fool, and that marriages between the old and the young invariably end in the divorce court (December *v.* May and July). She used to leave copies of a favourite Sunday newspaper on his table, where he could not fail to see the flaring headlines:

OLD MAN'S WEDDING ROMANCE
WIFE'S PERFIDY BRINGS GREY HAIR IN SORROW
TO THE LAW COURTS.

Whether Mr. Reeder perused these human documents she did not know. He never referred to the tragedies of ill-assorted unions, and went on meeting Miss Belman every morning at nine o'clock and at five-five in the afternoons whenever his business permitted.

He so rarely discussed his own business or introduced the subject that was exercising his mind that it was remarkable he should make even an oblique reference to his work. Possibly he would not have done so if Miss Margaret Belman had not introduced (unwillingly) a leader of conversation which traced indirectly to the disappearances.

They had been talking of holidays: Margaret was going to Cromer for a fortnight.

"I shall leave on the second. My monthly dividends (doesn't that sound grand?) are due on the first——"

"Eh?"

Reeder slued round. Dividends in most companies are paid at half-yearly intervals.

"Dividends, Miss Margaret?"

She flushed a little at his surprise and then laughed.

"You didn't realise that I was a woman of property?" she bantered him. "I receive ten pounds a month—my father left me a little house property when he died. I sold the cottages two years ago for a thousand pounds and found a wonderful investment."

Mr. Reeder made a rapid calculation.

"You are drawing something like 12½ per cent.," he said. "That is indeed a wonderful investment. What is the name of the company?"

She hesitated.

"I'm afraid I can't tell you that. You see—well, it's rather secret. It is to do with a South American syndicate that supplies arms to—what do you call them—insurgents! I know it is rather dreadful to make money that

97

way—I mean out of arms and things, but it pays terribly well and I can't afford to miss the opportunity.''

Reeder frowned.

"But why is it such a terrible secret?" he asked. "Quite a number of respectable people make money out of armament concerns."

Again she showed reluctance to explain her meaning.

"We are pledged—the shareholders, I mean—not to divulge our connection with the company," she said. "That is one of the agreements I had to sign. And the money comes regularly. I have had nearly £300 of my thousand back in dividends already."

"Humph!" said Mr. Reeder, wise enough not to press his question. There was another day to-morrow.

But the opportunity to which he looked forward on the following morning was denied to him. Somebody played a grim "joke" on him—the kind of joke to which he was accustomed, for there were men who had good reason to hate him, and never a year passed but one or the other sought to repay him for his unkindly attentions.

"Your name is Reeder, ain't it?"

Mr. Reeder, tightly grasping his umbrella with both hands, looked over his spectacles at the shabby man who stood at the bottom of the steps. He was on the point of leaving his house in the Brockley Road for his office in Whitehall, and since he was a methodical man and worked to a time table, he resented in his mild way this interruption which had already cost him fifteen seconds of valuable time.

"You're the fellow who shopped Ike Walker, ain't you?"

Mr. Reeder had indeed "shopped" many men. He was by profession a shopper, which, translated from the argot, means a man who procures the arrest of an evildoer. Ike Walker he knew very well indeed. He was a clever, a too clever, forger of bills of exchange, and was at that precise moment almost permanently employed as orderly in the convict prison at Dartmoor, and might account himself fortunate if he held this easy job for the rest of his twelve years' sentence.

His interrogator was a little hard-faced man wearing a suit that had evidently been originally intended for somebody of greater girth and more commanding height. His trousers were turned up noticeably; his waistcoat was full of folds and tucks which only an amateur tailor would have dared, and only one superior to the criticism of his fellows would have worn. His hard, bright eyes were fixed on Mr. Reeder, but there was no menace in them so far as the detective could read.

"Yes, I was instrumental in arresting Ike Walker," said Mr. Reeder, almost gently.

The man put his hand in his pocket and brought out a crumpled packet enclosed in green oiled silk. Mr. Reeder unfolded the covering and found a soiled and crumpled envelope.

"That's from Ike," said the man. "He sent it out of stir by a gent who was discharged yesterday."

Mr. Reeder was not shocked by his revelation. He knew that prison rules were made to be broken, and that worse things have happened in the best regulated jails than this item of a smuggled letter. He opened the envelope, keeping his eyes on the man's face, took out the crumpled sheet and read the five or six lines of writing.

DEAR REEDER:
Here is a bit of a riddle for you.
What other people have got, you can have. I haven't got it, but it is coming to you. It's red-hot when you get it, but you're cold when it goes away.

Your loving friend,

IKE WALKER

(doing a twelve stretch because you went on the witness stand and told a lot of lies).

Mr. Reeder looked up and their eyes met.

"Your friend is a little mad, one thinks?" he asked politely.

"He ain't a friend of mine. A gent asked me to bring it," said the messenger.

"On the contrary," said Mr. Reeder pleasantly, "he gave it to you in Dartmoor Prison yesterday. Your name is Mills; you have eight convictions for burglary, and will have your ninth before the year is out. You were released two days ago—I saw you reporting at Scotland Yard."

The man was for the moment alarmed and in two minds to bolt. Mr. Reeder glanced along Brockley Road, saw a slim figure, that was standing at the corner, cross to a waiting tramcar, and, seeing his opportunity vanish, readjusted his time table.

"Come inside, Mr. Mills."

"I don't want to come inside," said Mr. Mills, now thoroughly agitated. "He asked me to give this to you and I've give it. There's nothing else——"

Mr. Reeder crooked his finger.

"Come, birdie!" he said, with great amiability. "And please don't annoy me! I am quite capable of sending you back to your friend Mr. Walker. I am really a most unpleasant man if I am upset."

The messenger followed meekly, wiped his boots with great vigour on the mat and tiptoed up the carpeted stairs to the big study where Mr. Reeder did most of his thinking.

"Sit down, Mills."

With his own hands Mr. Reeder placed a chair for his uncomfortable visitor, and then, pulling another up to his big writing table, he spread the letter before him, adjusted his glasses, read, his lips moving, and then leaned back in his chair.

"I give it up," he said. "Read me this riddle."

"I don't know what's in the letter——" began the man.

"Read me this riddle."

As he handed the letter across the table, the man betrayed himself, for he rose and pushed back his chair with a startled, horrified expression that told Mr. Reeder quite a lot. He laid the letter down on his desk, took a large tumbler from the sideboard, inverted it and covered the scrawled paper. Then:

"Wait," he said, "and don't move till I come back."

And there was an unaccustomed venom in his tone that made the visitor shudder.

Reeder passed out of the room to the bathroom, pulled up his sleeves with a quick jerk of his arm and, turning the faucet, let hot water run over his hands before he reached for a small bottle on a shelf, poured a liberal portion into the water and let his hands soak. This done, for three minutes he scrubbed his fingers with a nail-brush, dried them, and, removing his coat and waistcoat carefully, hung them over the edge of the bath. He went back to his uncomfortable guest in his shirt-sleeves.

"Our friend Walker is employed in the hospital," he stated rather than asked. "What have you had there—scarlet fever or something worse?"

He glanced down at the letter under the glass.

"Scarlet fever, of course," he said, "and the letter has been systematically infected. Walker is almost clever."

The wood of a fire was laid in the grate. He carried the letter and the blotting-paper to the hearth, lit the kindling and thrust paper and letter into the flames.

"Almost clever," he said musingly. "Of course, he is one of the orderlies in the hospital. It was scarlet fever, I think you said?"

The gaping man nodded.

"Of a virulent type, of course. How very fascinating!"

He thrust his hands in his pockets and looked down benevolently at the wretched emissary of the vengeful Walker.

"You may go now, Mills," he said gently. "I rather think that you are infected. That ridiculous piece of oiled silk is quite inadequate—which means 'quite useless'—as a protection against wandering germs. You will have scarlet fever in three days, and will probably be dead at the end of the week. I will send you a wreath."

He opened the door, pointed to the stairway and the man slunk out.

Mr. Reeder watched him through the window, saw him cross the street and disappear round the corner into the Lewisham High Road, and then, going up to his bedroom, he put on a newer frock-coat and waistcoat, drew on his hands a pair of fabric gloves and went forth to his labours.

He did not expect to met Mr. Mills again, never dreaming that the gentleman from Dartmoor was planning a "bust" which would bring them again into contact. For Mr. Reeder the incident was closed.

That day news of another disappearance had come through from police headquarters, and Mr. Reeder was waiting at ten minutes before five at the rendezvous for the girl who, he instinctively knew, could give him a thread of the clue. He was determined that this time his inquiries should bear fruit; but it was not until they had reached the end of Brockley Road, and he was walking slowly up toward the girl's boarding-house, that she gave him a hint.

"Why are you so persistent, Mr. Reeder?" she asked, a little impatiently. "Do you wish to invest money? Because, if you do, I'm sorry I can't help you. That is another agreement we made, that we would not introduce new shareholders."

Mr. Reeder stopped, took off his hat and rubbed the back of his head (his housekeeper, watching him from an upper window, was perfectly certain he was proposing and had been rejected).

"I am going to tell you something, Miss Belman, and I hope—er—that I shall not alarm you."

And very briefly he told the story of the disappearances and the queer coincidence which marked every case—the receipt of a dividend on the first of every month. As he proceeded, the colour left the girl's face.

"You are serious, of course?" she said, serious enough herself. "You wouldn't tell me that unless——The company is the Mexico City Investment Syndicate. They have offices in Portugal Street."

"How did you come to hear of them?" asked Mr. Reeder.

"I had a letter from their manager, Mr. De Silvo. He told me that a friend had mentioned my name, and gave full particulars of the investment."

"Have you that letter?"

She shook her head.

"No; I was particularly asked to bring it with me when I went to see them. Although, in point of fact, I never did see them," smiled the girl. "I wrote to their lawyers—will you wait? I have their letter."

Mr. Reeder waited at the gate while the girl went into the house and returned presently with a small portfolio, from which she took a quarto sheet. It was headed with the name of a legal firm, Bracher & Bracher, and was the usual formal type of letter one expects from a lawyer.

DEAR MADAM:

Re Mexico City Investment Syndicate: We act as lawyers to this syndicate, and so far as we know it is a reputable concern. We feel that it is only due to us that we should say that we do not advise investments in any concern which offers such large profits, for usually there is a corresponding risk. We know, however, that this syndicate has paid 12½ per cent. and sometimes as much as 20 per cent., and we have had no complaints about them. We cannot, of course, as lawyers, guarantee the financial soundness of any of our clients, and can only repeat that, in so far as we have been able to ascertain, the syndicate conducts a genuine business and enjoys a very sound financial backing.

Yours faithfully,
BRACHER & BRACHER.

"You say you never saw De Silvo?"

She shook her head.

"No; I saw Mr. Bracher, but when I went to the office of the syndicate, which is in the same building, I found only a clerk in attendance. Mr. De Silvo had been called out of town. I had to leave the letter because the lower portion was an application for shares in the syndicate. The capital could be withdrawn at three days' notice, and I must say that this last clause decided me; and when I had a letter from Mr. De Silvo accepting my investment, I sent him the money."

Mr. Reeder nodded.

"And you've received your dividends regularly ever since?" he said.

"Every month," said the girl triumphantly. "And really I think you're wrong in connecting the company with these disappearances."

Mr. Reeder did not reply. That afternoon he made it his business to call at 179 Portugal Street. It was a two-story building of an old-fashioned type. A wide flagged hall led into the building; a set of old-fashioned stairs ran up to the "top floor," which was occupied by a China merchant; and from the hall led three doors. That on the left bore the legend "Bracher & Bracher, Solicitors," and immediately facing was the office of the Mexican syndicate. At the far end of the passage was a door which exhibited the name "John Baston," but as to Mr. Baston's business there was no indication.

Mr. Reeder knocked gently at the door of the syndicate and a voice bade him come in. A young man, wearing glasses, was sitting at a typewriting table, a pair of dictaphone receivers in his ears, and he was typing rapidly.

"No, sir, Mr. De Silvo is not in. He only comes in about twice a week," said the clerk. "Will you give me your name?"

"It is not important," said Reeder gently, and went out, closing the door behind him.

He was more fortunate in his call upon Bracher & Bracher, for Mr.

Joseph Bracher was in his office: a tall, florid gentleman who wore a large rose in his buttonhole. The firm of Bracher & Bracher was evidently a prosperous one, for there were half a dozen clerks in the outer office, and Mr. Bracher's private sanctum, with its big partner desk, was a model of shabby comfort.

"Sit down, Mr. Reeder," said the lawyer, glancing at the card.

In a few words Mr. Reeder stated his business, and Mr. Bracher smiled.

"It is fortunate you came to-day," he said. "If it were to-morrow we should not be able to give you any information. The truth is, we have had to ask Mr. De Silvo to find other lawyers. No, no, there is nothing wrong, except that they constantly refer their clients to us, and we feel that we are becoming in the nature of sponsors for their clients, and that, of course, is very undesirable."

"Have you a record of the people who have written to you from time to time asking your advice?"

Mr. Bracher shook his head.

"It is a curious thing to confess, but we haven't," he said; "and that is one of the reasons why we have decided to give up this client. Three weeks ago, the letter-book in which we kept copies of all letters sent to people who applied for a reference most unaccountably disappeared. It was put in the safe overnight, and in the morning, although there was no sign of tampering with the lock, it had vanished. The circumstances were so mysterious, and my brother and I were so deeply concerned, that we applied to the syndicate to give us a list of their clients, and that request was never complied with."

Mr. Reeder sought inspiration in the ceiling.

"Who is John Baston?" he asked, and the lawyer laughed.

"There again I am ignorant. I believe he is a very wealthy financier, but, so far as I know, he only comes to his office for three months in the year, and I have never seen him."

Mr. Reeder offered him his flabby hand and walked back along Portugal Street, his chin on his breast, his hands behind him dragging his umbrella, so that he bore a ludicrous resemblance to some strange tailed animal.

That night he waited again for the girl, but she did not appear, and although he remained at the rendezvous until half-past five he did not see her. This was not very unusual, for sometimes she had to work late, and he went home without any feeling of apprehension. He finished his own frugal dinner and then walked across to the boarding-house. Miss Belman had not arrived, the landlady told him, and he returned to his study and telephoned first to the office where she was employed and then to the private address of her employer.

"She left at half-past four," was the surprising news. "Somebody telephoned to her and she asked me if she might go early."

"Oh!" said Mr. Reeder blankly.

He did not go to bed that night, but sat up in a small room at Scotland Yard, reading the brief reports which came in from the various divisions. And with the morning came the sickening realisation that Margaret Belman's name must be added to those who had disappeared in such extraordinary circumstances.

He dozed in the big Windsor chair. At eight o'clock he returned to his own house and shaved and bathed, and when the Public Prosecutor arrived at his office he found Mr. Reeder waiting for him in the corridor. It was a changed Mr. Reeder, and the change was not due entirely to lack of sleep. His voice was sharper; he had lost some of that atmosphere of apology which usually enveloped him.

In a few words he told of Margaret Belman's disappearance.

"Do you connect De Silvo with this?" asked his chief.

"Yes, I think I do," said the other quietly, and then: "There is only one hope, and it is a very slender one—a very slender one indeed!"

He did not tell the Public Prosecutor in what that hope consisted, but walked down to the offices of the Mexico City Investment Syndicate.

Mr. De Silvo was not in. He would have been very much surprised if he had been. He crossed the hallway to see the lawyer, and this time he found Mr. Ernest Bracher present with his brother.

When Reeder spoke to the point, it was very much to the point.

"I am leaving a police officer in Portugal Street to arrest De Silvo the moment he puts in an appearance. I feel that you, as his lawyers, should know this," he said.

"But why on earth——?" began Mr. Joseph Bracher, in a tone of astonishment.

"I don't know what charge I shall bring against him, but it will certainly be a very serious one," said Reeder. "For the moment I have not confided to Scotland Yard the basis for my suspicions, but your client has got to tell a very plausible story and produce indisputable proof of his innocence to have any hope of escape."

"I am quite in the dark," said the lawyer, mystified. "What has he been doing? Is his syndicate a fraud?"

"I know nothing more fraudulent," said the other shortly. "To-morrow I intend to obtain the necessary authority to search his papers and to search the room and papers of Mr. John Baston. I have an idea that I shall find something in that room of considerable interest to me."

It was eight o'clock that night before he left Scotland Yard, and he was turning toward the familiar corner, when he saw a car come from Westminster Bridge toward Scotland Yard. Somebody leaned out of the window and signalled him, and the car turned. It was a two-seater coupé and the driver was Mr. Joseph Bracher.

"We've found De Silvo," he said breathlessly as he brought the car to a standstill at the curb and jumped out.

He was very agitated and his face was pale. Mr. Reeder could have sworn that his teeth were chattering.

"There's something wrong—very badly wrong," he went on. "My brother has been trying to get the truth from him—my God! if he has done these terrible things I shall never forgive myself."

"Where is he?" asked Mr. Reeder.

"He came just before dinner to our house at Dulwich. My brother and I are bachelors and we live there alone now, and he has been to dinner before. My brother questioned him and he made certain admissions which are almost incredible. The man must be mad."

"What did he say?"

"I can't tell you. Ernest is detaining him until you come."

Mr. Reeder stepped into the car and in a few minutes they were flying across Westminster Bridge toward Camberwell. Lane House, an old-fashioned Georgian residence, lay at the end of a countrified road which was, he found, a cul de sac. The house stood in grounds of considerable size, he noted as they passed up the drive and stopped before the porch. Mr. Bracher alighted and opened the door, and Reeder passed into a cosily furnished hall. One door was ajar.

"Is that Mr. Reeder?" He recognised the voice of Ernest Bracher, and walked into the room.

The younger Mr. Bracher was standing with his back to the empty fireplace; there was nobody else in the room.

"De Silvo's gone upstairs to lie down," explained the lawyer. "This is a dreadful business, Mr. Reeder."

He held out his hand and Reeder crossed the room to take it. As he put his foot on the square Persian rug before the fireplace, he realised his danger and tried to spring back, but his balance was lost. He felt himself falling through the cavity which the carpet hid, lashed out and caught for a moment the edge of the trap, but as the lawyer came round and raised his foot to stamp upon the clutching fingers, Reeder released his hold and dropped.

The shock of the fall took away his breath, and for a second he sprawled, half lying, half sitting, on the floor of the cellar into which he had fallen. Looking up, he saw the older of the two leaning over. The square aperture was diminishing in size. There was evidently a sliding panel which covered the hole in normal times.

"We'll deal with you later, Reeder," said Joseph Bracher with a smile. "We've had quite a lot of clever people here——"

Something cracked in the cellar. The bullet seared the lawyer's cheek, smashed a glass chandelier to fragments, and he stepped back with a yell of fear. In another second the trap was closed and Reeder was alone in a small brick-lined cellar. Not entirely alone, for the automatic pistol he held in his hand was a very pleasant companion in that moment of crisis.

From his hip pocket he took a flat electric hand-lamp, switched on the current and surveyed his prison. The walls and floor were damp; that was the first thing he noticed. In one corner was a small flight of brick steps leading to a locked steel door, and then:

"Mr. Reeder."

He spun round and turned his lamp upon the speaker. It was Margaret Belman, who had risen from a heap of sacks where she had been sleeping.

"I'm afraid I've got you into very bad trouble," she said, and he marvelled at her calm.

"How long have you been here?"

"Since last night," she answered. "Mr. Bracher telephoned me to see him and he picked me up in his car. They kept me in the other room until to-night, but an hour ago they brought me here."

"Which is the other room?"

She pointed to the steel door. She offered no further details of her capture, and it was not a moment to discuss their misfortune. Reeder went up the steps and tried the door; it was fastened from the other side, and opened inward, he discovered. There was no sign of a keyhole. He asked her where the door led and she told him that it was to an underground kitchen and coal-cellar. She had hoped to escape, because only a barred window stood between her and freedom in the "little room" where she was kept.

"But the window was very thick," she said, "and of course I could do nothing with the bars."

Reeder made another inspection of the cellar, then sent the light of his lamp up at the ceiling. He saw nothing there except a steel pulley fastened to a beam that crossed the entire width of the cellar.

"Now what on earth is he going to do?" he asked thoughtfully, and as though his enemies had heard the question and were determined to leave him in no doubt as to their plans, there came the sound of gurgling water, and in a second he was ankle-deep.

He put the light on to the place whence the water was coming. There were three circular holes in the wall, from each of which was gushing a solid stream.

"What is it?" she asked in a terrified whisper.

"Get on to the steps and stay there," he ordered peremptorily, and made investigation to see if it was possible to staunch the flow. He saw at a glance that this was impossible. And now the mystery of the disappearances was a mystery no longer.

The water came up with incredible rapidity, first to his knees, then to his thighs, and he joined her on the steps.

There was no possible escape for them. He guessed the water would come up only so far as would make it impossible for them to reach the beam across the roof or the pulley, the dreadful purpose of which he could guess. The dead must be got out of this charnel house in some way or other. Strong swimmer as he was, he knew that in the hours ahead it would be impossible to keep afloat.

He slipped off his coat and vest and unbuttoned his collar.

"You had better take off your skirt," he said in a matter-of-fact tone. "Can you swim?"

"Yes," she answered in a low voice.

He did not ask her the real question which was in his mind: for how long could she swim?

There was a long silence; the water crept higher; and then:

"Are you very much afraid?" he asked, and took her hand in his.

"No, I don't think I am," she said. "It is wonderful having you with me—why are they doing this?"

He said nothing, but carried the soft hand to his lips and kissed it.

The water was now reaching the top step. Reeder stood with his back to the iron door, waiting. And then he felt something touch the door from the other side. There was a faint click, as though a bolt had been slipped back. He put her gently aside and held his palms to the door. There was no doubt now: somebody was fumbling on the other side. He went down a step and presently he felt the door yield and come toward him, and there was a momentary gleam of light. In another second he had wrenched the door open and sprung through.

"Hands up!"

Whoever it was had dropped his lamp, and now Mr. Reeder focussed the light of his own torch and nearly dropped.

For the man in the passage was Mills, the ex-convict who had brought the tainted letter from Dartmoor!

"All right, guv'nor, it's a cop," growled the man.

And then the whole explanation flashed upon the detective. In an instant he had gripped the girl by the hand and dragged her through the narrow passage, into which the water was now steadily overrunning.

"Which way did you get in, Mills?" he demanded authoritatively.

"Through the window."

"Show me—quick!"

The convict led the way to what was evidently the window through which the girl had looked with such longing. The bars had been removed; the window sash itself lifted from its rusty hinges; and in another second the three were standing on the grass, with the stars twinkling above them.

"Mills," said Mr. Reeder, and his voice shook, "you came here to 'bust' this house."

"That's right," growled Mills. "I tell you it's a cop. I'm not going to give you any trouble."

"Skip!" hissed Mr. Reeder. "And skip quick! Now, young lady, we'll go for a little walk."

A few seconds later a patrolling constable was smitten dumb by the apparition of a middle-aged man in shirt and trousers, and a lady who was inadequately attired in a silk petticoat.

*　　*　　*　　*　　*

"The Mexican company was Bracher & Bracher," explained Reeder to his chief. "There was no John Baston. His room was a passage-way by which the Brachers could get from one room to the other. The clerk in the Mexican syndicate's office was, of course, blind; I spotted that the moment I saw him. There are any number of blind typists employed in the City of London. A blind clerk was necessary if the identity of De Silvo with the Brachers was to be kept a secret.

"Bracher & Bracher had been going badly for years. It will probably be found that they have made away with clients' money; and they hit upon this scheme of inducing foolish investors to put money into their syndicate on the promise of large dividends. Their victims were well chosen, and Joseph—who was the brains of the organisation—conducted the most rigorous investigation to make sure that these unfortunate people had no intimate friends. If they had any suspicion about an applicant, Brachers would write a letter deprecating the idea of an investment and suggesting that the too-shrewd dupe should find another and a safer method than the Mexican syndicate afforded.

"After they had paid one or two years' dividends the wretched investor was lured to the house at Dulwich and there scientifically killed. You will probably find an unofficial cemetery in their grounds. So far as I can make out, they have stolen more than a hundred and twenty thousand pounds in the past two years by this method."

"It is incredible," said the Prosecutor, "incredible!"

Mr. Reeder shrugged.

"Is there anything more incredible than the Burke and Hare murders? There are Burkes and Hares in every branch of society and in every period of history."

"Why did they delay their execution of Miss Belman?"

Mr. Reeder coughed.

"They wanted to make a clean sweep, but did not wish to kill her until they had me in their hands. I rather suspect"—he coughed again—"that they thought I had an especial interest in the young lady."

"And have you?" asked the Public Prosecutor.

Mr. Reeder did not reply.

A CATALOGUE OF
SELECTED DOVER BOOKS
IN ALL FIELDS OF INTEREST

A CATALOGUE OF SELECTED DOVER
BOOKS IN ALL FIELDS OF INTEREST

RACKHAM'S COLOR ILLUSTRATIONS FOR WAGNER'S RING. Rackham's finest mature work—all 64 full-color watercolors in a faithful and lush interpretation of the *Ring*. Full-sized plates on coated stock of the paintings used by opera companies for authentic staging of Wagner. Captions aid in following complete Ring cycle. Introduction. 64 illustrations plus vignettes. 72pp. 8⅝ x 11¼.   23779-6 Pa. $6.00

CONTEMPORARY POLISH POSTERS IN FULL COLOR, edited by Joseph Czestochowski. 46 full-color examples of brilliant school of Polish graphic design, selected from world's first museum (near Warsaw) dedicated to poster art. Posters on circuses, films, plays, concerts all show cosmopolitan influences, free imagination. Introduction. 48pp. 9⅜ x 12¼.
                                                     23780-X Pa. $6.00

GRAPHIC WORKS OF EDVARD MUNCH, Edvard Munch. 90 haunting, evocative prints by first major Expressionist artist and one of the greatest graphic artists of his time: *The Scream, Anxiety, Death Chamber, The Kiss, Madonna*, etc. Introduction by Alfred Werner. 90pp. 9 x 12.
                                                     23765-6 Pa. $5.00

THE GOLDEN AGE OF THE POSTER, Hayward and Blanche Cirker. 70 extraordinary posters in full colors, from Maitres de l'Affiche, Mucha, Lautrec, Bradley, Cheret, Beardsley, many others. Total of 78pp. 9⅜ x 12¼.   22753-7 Pa. $5.95

THE NOTEBOOKS OF LEONARDO DA VINCI, edited by J. P. Richter. Extracts from manuscripts reveal great genius; on painting, sculpture, anatomy, sciences, geography, etc. Both Italian and English. 186 ms. pages reproduced, plus 500 additional drawings, including studies for *Last Supper*, Sforza monument, etc. 860pp. 7⅞ x 10¾. (Available in U.S. only)
                               22572-0, 22573-9 Pa., Two-vol. set $15.90

THE CODEX NUTTALL, as first edited by Zelia Nuttall. Only inexpensive edition, in full color, of a pre-Columbian Mexican (Mixtec) book. 88 color plates show kings, gods, heroes, temples, sacrifices. New explanatory, historical introduction by Arthur G. Miller. 96pp. 11⅜ x 8½. (Available in U.S. only)   23168-2 Pa. $7.95

UNE SEMAINE DE BONTÉ, A SURREALISTIC NOVEL IN COLLAGE, Max Ernst. Masterpiece created out of 19th-century periodical illustrations, explores worlds of terror and surprise. Some consider this Ernst's greatest work. 208pp. 8⅛ x 11.   23252-2 Pa. $6.00

THE AMERICAN SENATOR, Anthony Trollope. Little known, long unavailable Trollope novel on a grand scale. Here are humorous comment on American vs. English culture, and stunning portrayal of a heroine/villainess. Superb evocation of Victorian village life. 561pp. 5⅜ x 8½.
23801-6 Pa. $6.00

WAS IT MURDER? James Hilton. The author of *Lost Horizon* and *Goodbye, Mr. Chips* wrote one detective novel (under a pen-name) which was quickly forgotten and virtually lost, even at the height of Hilton's fame. This edition brings it back—a finely crafted public school puzzle resplendent with Hilton's stylish atmosphere. A thoroughly English thriller by the creator of Shangri-la. 252pp. 5⅜ x 8. (Available in U.S. only)
23774-5 Pa. $3.00

CENTRAL PARK: A PHOTOGRAPHIC GUIDE, Victor Laredo and Henry Hope Reed. 121 superb photographs show dramatic views of Central Park: Bethesda Fountain, Cleopatra's Needle, Sheep Meadow, the Blockhouse, plus people engaged in many park activities: ice skating, bike riding, etc. Captions by former Curator of Central Park, Henry Hope Reed, provide historical view, changes, etc. Also photos of N.Y. landmarks on park's periphery. 96pp. 8½ x 11. 23750-8 Pa. $4.50

NANTUCKET IN THE NINETEENTH CENTURY, Clay Lancaster. 180 rare photographs, stereographs, maps, drawings and floor plans recreate unique American island society. Authentic scenes of shipwreck, lighthouses, streets, homes are arranged in geographic sequence to provide walking-tour guide to old Nantucket existing today. Introduction, captions. 160pp. 8⅞ x 11¾. 23747-8 Pa. $6.95

STONE AND MAN: A PHOTOGRAPHIC EXPLORATION, Andreas Feininger. 106 photographs by *Life* photographer Feininger portray man's deep passion for stone through the ages. Stonehenge-like megaliths, fortified towns, sculpted marble and crumbling tenements show textures, beauties, fascination. 128pp. 9¼ x 10¾. 23756-7 Pa. $5.95

CIRCLES, A MATHEMATICAL VIEW, D. Pedoe. Fundamental aspects of college geometry, non-Euclidean geometry, and other branches of mathematics: representing circle by point. Poincare model, isoperimetric property, etc. Stimulating recreational reading. 66 figures. 96pp. 5⅝ x 8¼.
63698-4 Pa. $2.75

THE DISCOVERY OF NEPTUNE, Morton Grosser. Dramatic scientific history of the investigations leading up to the actual discovery of the eighth planet of our solar system. Lucid, well-researched book by well-known historian of science. 172pp. 5⅜ x 8½. 23726-5 Pa. $3.50

THE DEVIL'S DICTIONARY. Ambrose Bierce. Barbed, bitter, brilliant witticisms in the form of a dictionary. Best, most ferocious satire America has produced. 145pp. 5⅜ x 8½. 20487-1 Pa. $2.25

"OSCAR" OF THE WALDORF'S COOKBOOK, Oscar Tschirky. Famous American chef reveals 3455 recipes that made Waldorf great; cream of French, German, American cooking, in all categories. Full instructions, easy home use. 1896 edition. 907pp. 6⅝ x 9⅜.   20790-0 Clothbd. $15.00

COOKING WITH BEER, Carole Fahy. Beer has as superb an effect on food as wine, and at fraction of cost. Over 250 recipes for appetizers, soups, main dishes, desserts, breads, etc. Index. 144pp. 5⅜ x 8½. (Available in U.S. only)   23661-7 Pa. $2.50

STEWS AND RAGOUTS, Kay Shaw Nelson. This international cookbook offers wide range of 108 recipes perfect for everyday, special occasions, meals-in-themselves, main dishes. Economical, nutritious, easy-to-prepare: goulash, Irish stew, boeuf bourguignon, etc. Index. 134pp. 5⅜ x 8½.
                                                                23662-5 Pa. $2.50

DELICIOUS MAIN COURSE DISHES, Marian Tracy. Main courses are the most important part of any meal. These 200 nutritious, economical recipes from around the world make every meal a delight. "I . . . have found it so useful in my own household,"—N.Y. Times. Index. 219pp. 5⅜ x 8½.   23664-1 Pa. $3.00

FIVE ACRES AND INDEPENDENCE, Maurice G. Kains. Great back-to-the-land classic explains basics of self-sufficient farming: economics, plants, crops, animals, orchards, soils, land selection, host of other necessary things. Do not confuse with skimpy faddist literature; Kains was one of America's greatest agriculturalists. 95 illustrations. 397pp. 5⅜ x 8½.
                                                                20974-1 Pa.$3.95

A PRACTICAL GUIDE FOR THE BEGINNING FARMER, Herbert Jacobs. Basic, extremely useful first book for anyone thinking about moving to the country and starting a farm. Simpler than Kains, with greater emphasis on country living in general. 246pp. 5⅜ x 8½.
                                                                23675-7 Pa. $3.50

PAPERMAKING, Dard Hunter. Definitive book on the subject by the foremost authority in the field. Chapters dealing with every aspect of history of craft in every part of the world. Over 320 illustrations. 2nd, revised and enlarged (1947) edition. 672pp. 5⅜ x 8½.   23619-6 Pa. $7.95

THE ART DECO STYLE, edited by Theodore Menten. Furniture, jewelry, metalwork, ceramics, fabrics, lighting fixtures, interior decors, exteriors, graphics from pure French sources. Best sampling around. Over 400 photographs. 183pp. 8⅜ x 11¼.   22824-X Pa. $6.00

ACKERMANN'S COSTUME PLATES, Rudolph Ackermann. Selection of 96 plates from the Repository of Arts, best published source of costume for English fashion during the early 19th century. 12 plates also in color. Captions, glossary and introduction by editor Stella Blum. Total of 120pp. 8⅜ x 11¼.   23690-0 Pa. $4.50

UNCLE SILAS, J. Sheridan LeFanu. Victorian Gothic mystery novel, considered by many best of period, even better than Collins or Dickens. Wonderful psychological terror. Introduction by Frederick Shroyer. 436pp. 5⅜ x 8½. 21715-9 Pa. $6.00

JURGEN, James Branch Cabell. The great erotic fantasy of the 1920's that delighted thousands, shocked thousands more. Full final text, Lane edition with 13 plates by Frank Pape. 346pp. 5⅜ x 8½. 23507-6 Pa. $4.50

THE CLAVERINGS, Anthony Trollope. Major novel, chronicling aspects of British Victorian society, personalities. Reprint of Cornhill serialization, 16 plates by M. Edwards; first reprint of full text. Introduction by Norman Donaldson. 412pp. 5⅜ x 8½. 23464-9 Pa. $5.00

KEPT IN THE DARK, Anthony Trollope. Unusual short novel about Victorian morality and abnormal psychology by the great English author. Probably the first American publication. Frontispiece by Sir John Millais. 92pp. 6½ x 9¼. 23609-9 Pa. $2.50

RALPH THE HEIR, Anthony Trollope. Forgotten tale of illegitimacy, inheritance. Master novel of Trollope's later years. Victorian country estates, clubs, Parliament, fox hunting, world of fully realized characters. Reprint of 1871 edition. 12 illustrations by F. A. Faser. 434pp. of text. 5⅜ x 8½. 23642-0 Pa. $5.00

YEKL and THE IMPORTED BRIDEGROOM AND OTHER STORIES OF THE NEW YORK GHETTO, Abraham Cahan. Film *Hester Street* based on *Yekl* (1896). Novel, other stories among first about Jewish immigrants of N.Y.'s East Side. Highly praised by W. D. Howells—Cahan "a new star of realism." New introduction by Bernard G. Richards. 240pp. 5⅜ x 8½. 22427-9 Pa. $3.50

THE HIGH PLACE, James Branch Cabell. Great fantasy writer's enchanting comedy of disenchantment set in 18th-century France. Considered by some critics to be even better than his famous *Jurgen*. 10 illustrations and numerous vignettes by noted fantasy artist Frank C. Pape. 320pp. 5⅜ x 8½. 23670-6 Pa. $4.00

ALICE'S ADVENTURES UNDER GROUND, Lewis Carroll. Facsimile of ms. Carroll gave Alice Liddell in 1864. Different in many ways from final Alice. Handlettered, illustrated by Carroll. Introduction by Martin Gardner. 128pp. 5⅜ x 8½. 21482-6 Pa. $2.50

FAVORITE ANDREW LANG FAIRY TALE BOOKS IN MANY COLORS, Andrew Lang. The four Lang favorites in a boxed set—the complete *Red, Green, Yellow* and *Blue* Fairy Books. 164 stories; 439 illustrations by Lancelot Speed, Henry Ford and G. P. Jacomb Hood. Total of about 1500pp. 5⅜ x 8½. 23407-X Boxed set, Pa. $15.95

HOUSEHOLD STORIES BY THE BROTHERS GRIMM. All the great Grimm stories: "Rumpelstiltskin," "Snow White," "Hansel and Gretel," etc., with 114 illustrations by Walter Crane. 269pp. 5⅜ x 8½.
21080-4 Pa. $3.50

SLEEPING BEAUTY, illustrated by Arthur Rackham. Perhaps the fullest, most delightful version ever, told by C. S. Evans. Rackham's best work. 49 illustrations. 110pp. 7⅞ x 10¾. 22756-1 Pa. $2.50

AMERICAN FAIRY TALES, L. Frank Baum. Young cowboy lassoes Father Time; dummy in Mr. Floman's department store window comes to life; and 10 other fairy tales. 41 illustrations by N. P. Hall, Harry Kennedy, Ike Morgan, and Ralph Gardner. 209pp. 5⅜ x 8½. 23643-9 Pa. $3.00

THE WONDERFUL WIZARD OF OZ, L. Frank Baum. Facsimile in full color of America's finest children's classic. Introduction by Martin Gardner. 143 illustrations by W. W. Denslow. 267pp. 5⅜ x 8½.
20691-2 Pa. $3.50

THE TALE OF PETER RABBIT, Beatrix Potter. The inimitable Peter's terrifying adventure in Mr. McGregor's garden, with all 27 wonderful, full-color Potter illustrations. 55pp. 4¼ x 5½. (Available in U.S. only)
22827-4 Pa. $1.25

THE STORY OF KING ARTHUR AND HIS KNIGHTS, Howard Pyle. Finest children's version of life of King Arthur. 48 illustrations by Pyle. 131pp. 6⅛ x 9¼. 21445-1 Pa. $4.95

CARUSO'S CARICATURES, Enrico Caruso. Great tenor's remarkable caricatures of self, fellow musicians, composers, others. Toscanini, Puccini, Farrar, etc. Impish, cutting, insightful. 473 illustrations. Preface by M. Sisca. 217pp. 8⅜ x 11¼. 23528-9 Pa. $6.95

PERSONAL NARRATIVE OF A PILGRIMAGE TO ALMADINAH AND MECCAH, Richard Burton. Great travel classic by remarkably colorful personality. Burton, disguised as a Moroccan, visited sacred shrines of Islam, narrowly escaping death. Wonderful observations of Islamic life, customs, personalities. 47 illustrations. Total of 959pp. 5⅜ x 8½.
21217-3, 21218-1 Pa., Two-vol. set $12.00

INCIDENTS OF TRAVEL IN YUCATAN, John L. Stephens. Classic (1843) exploration of jungles of Yucatan, looking for evidences of Maya civilization. Travel adventures, Mexican and Indian culture, etc. Total of 669pp. 5⅜ x 8½. 20926-1, 20927-X Pa., Two-vol. set $7.90

AMERICAN LITERARY AUTOGRAPHS FROM WASHINGTON IRVING TO HENRY JAMES, Herbert Cahoon, et al. Letters, poems, manuscripts of Hawthorne, Thoreau, Twain, Alcott, Whitman, 67 other prominent American authors. Reproductions, full transcripts and commentary. Plus checklist of all American Literary Autographs in The Pierpont Morgan Library. Printed on exceptionally high-quality paper. 136 illustrations. 212pp. 9⅛ x 12¼. 23548-3 Pa. $12.50

AMERICAN ANTIQUE FURNITURE, Edgar G. Miller, Jr. The basic coverage of all American furniture before 1840: chapters per item chronologically cover all types of furniture, with more than 2100 photos. Total of 1106pp. 7⅞ x 10¾.   21599-7, 21600-4 Pa., Two-vol. set $17.90

ILLUSTRATED GUIDE TO SHAKER FURNITURE, Robert Meader. Director, Shaker Museum, Old Chatham, presents up-to-date coverage of all furniture and appurtenances, with much on local styles not available elsewhere. 235 photos. 146pp. 9 x 12.   22819-3 Pa. $6.00

ORIENTAL RUGS, ANTIQUE AND MODERN, Walter A. Hawley. Persia, Turkey, Caucasus, Central Asia, China, other traditions. Best general survey of all aspects: styles and periods, manufacture, uses, symbols and their interpretation, and identification. 96 illustrations, 11 in color. 320pp. 6⅛ x 9¼.   22366-3 Pa. $6.95

CHINESE POTTERY AND PORCELAIN, R. L. Hobson. Detailed descriptions and analyses by former Keeper of the Department of Oriental Antiquities and Ethnography at the British Museum. Covers hundreds of pieces from primitive times to 1915. Still the standard text for most periods. 136 plates, 40 in full color. Total of 750pp. 5⅜ x 8½.
23253-0 Pa. $10.00

THE WARES OF THE MING DYNASTY, R. L. Hobson. Foremost scholar examines and illustrates many varieties of Ming (1368-1644). Famous blue and white, polychrome, lesser-known styles and shapes. 117 illustrations, 9 full color, of outstanding pieces. Total of 263pp. 6⅛ x 9¼. (Available in U.S. only)   23652-8 Pa. $6.00

Prices subject to change without notice.

Available at your book dealer or write for free catalogue to Dept. GI, Dover Publications, Inc., 180 Varick St., N.Y., N.Y. 10014. Dover publishes more than 175 books each year on science, elementary and advanced mathematics, biology, music, art, literary history, social sciences and other areas.